E.D. HACKETT

The Havoc in My Head
Based on True Events

*Janice,
Enjoy!
EDHackett*

E.D. Hackett
Fiction Writer

IT'S THE LITTLE THINGS

First published by E.D. Hackett 2020

Copyright © 2020 by E.D. Hackett

All rights reserved. No part of this publication may be reproduced, stored or transmitted in any form or by any means, electronic, mechanical, photocopying, recording, scanning, or otherwise without written permission from the publisher. It is illegal to copy this book, post it to a website, or distribute it by any other means without permission.

This novel is entirely a work of fiction. The names, characters and incidents portrayed in it are the work of the author's imagination. Any resemblance to actual persons, living or dead, events or localities is entirely coincidental.

E.D. Hackett asserts the moral right to be identified as the author of this work.

Designations used by companies to distinguish their products are often claimed as trademarks. All brand names and product names used in this book and on its cover are trade names, service marks, trademarks and registered trademarks of their respective owners. The publishers and the book are not associated with any product or vendor mentioned in this book. None of the companies referenced within the book have endorsed the book.

Cover Art by 100 Covers

Second edition

This book was professionally typeset on Reedsy.
Find out more at reedsy.com

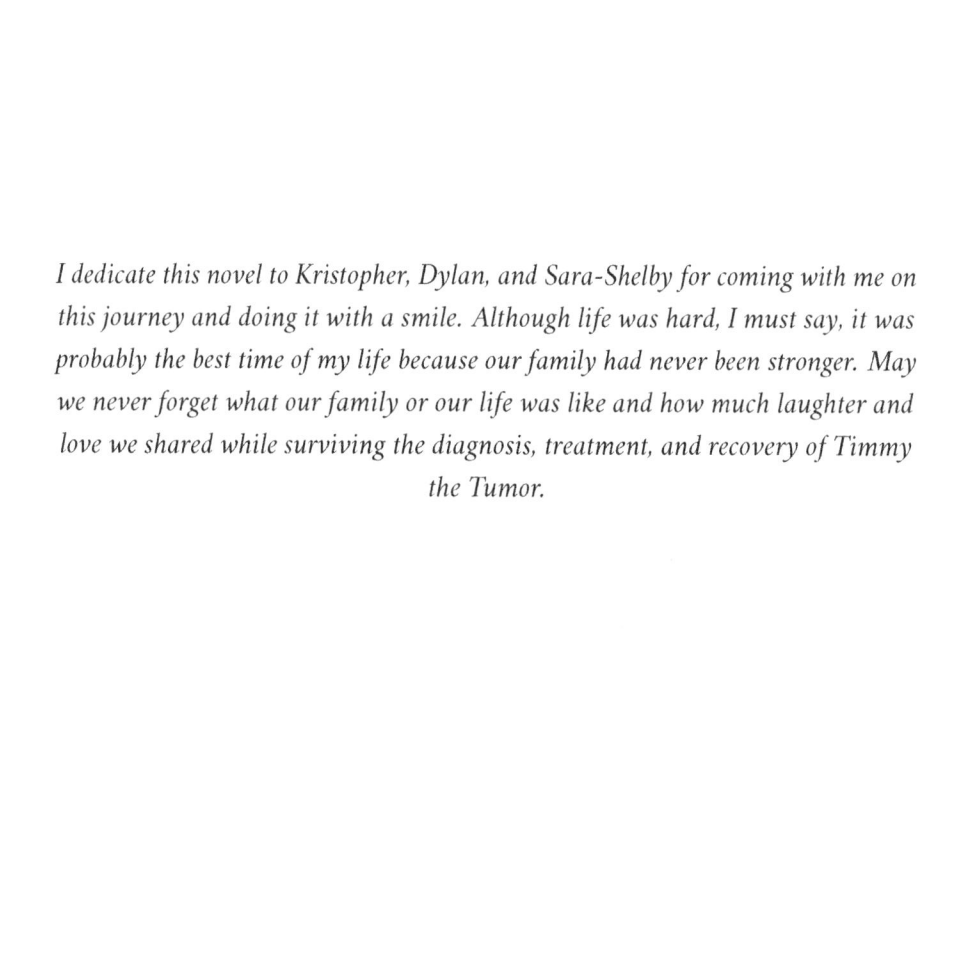

I dedicate this novel to Kristopher, Dylan, and Sara-Shelby for coming with me on this journey and doing it with a smile. Although life was hard, I must say, it was probably the best time of my life because our family had never been stronger. May we never forget what our family or our life was like and how much laughter and love we shared while surviving the diagnosis, treatment, and recovery of Timmy the Tumor.

Acknowledgement

Thank you to all the family and friends who came to my aid for those long ten months when I was out of work. My family and I are beyond grateful for the abundance of food, flowers, gift cards, and childcare.

I would also like to thank Andrea for being the first friend I confided my symptoms to on that very first day of work. Thank you for supporting me and listening to me every step of the way. Thank you for being the first person to read my novel. Your support and friendship are something I will always cherish.

To Maryann, for being there from the moment I was diagnosed to the last day of my radiation. You have been my rock throughout this whole ordeal.

Thank you to the Pituitary Tumor Support group. I probably wouldn't have survived this without your constant outpouring of love and advice. My goal when writing this book was to provide insight into this invisible disease.

Lastly, thank you to MGH and all the doctors who cared for me. I know I was at the best hospital for my diagnosis, and I will never forget the kindness, compassion, and stellar care provided.

Love, Edy.

Part One

When life shatters at your feet, remember to step delicately and breathe.
—E.D. Hackett

Chapter 1

"What if you have a brain tumor?" My best friend Jessica sipped her coffee, and looked at me with concern in her eyes. Her pursed lips and raised eyebrows waited for a response.

"What? No! It's just migraines. Doesn't everyone get migraines now and then?" I asked.

Jessica ran her finger up and down the beige coffee cup and placed it on the napkin that read "Marty's Diner." She put it on the booth table next to her half-eaten breakfast. "Yes, of course, people get headaches, but Ashley, you never had headaches before. Now you get one, and you are practically dead and despondent for the next twenty-four hours."

I hid a smile at her over-dramatic assumption. I knew my body handled stress differently than it had in the past, but life was different now. I had two children to take care of, an impossible job that allowed us to live in a beautiful gated community, and a husband who worked a side hustle for fun. He was living his best life while I paid most of the bills, but I loved that responsibility of providing for my family. I thought about money and schedules in my spare time, but as my kids got older, I questioned if my obsession with work was doing right by my family.

"Carefree and Spontaneous Ashley," a woman I used to know in college, quickly became "Coffee-Addicted Anxious Ashley" when my family grew to three and four. Migraines were part of the package, and I had managed to cope. "Yes, I get headaches, but it isn't every day. I do not have a brain tumor," I replied with certainty.

I picked up my coffee cup and stared out the window. The colorful leaves dotted the brown grass like paint splatter. The red, yellow, and orange leaves immersed themselves into each other to create one beautiful backdrop. A steady stream of cool air traveled through the gap in the old, dusty window and tiny goose pimples sprung upon my bare arm. I shivered in response and wrapped my new cashmere scarf tighter across my neck.

"Just keep track of your symptoms," Jessica said. "Sometimes these things happen when you least expect them."

I thought back to the first migraine I had experienced. I recalled studying in the tiny kitchen in my apartment during college. Living with three strangers, we had turned our living room into a bedroom to maximize our privacy, and I didn't consider any of them friends.

That day, I sat at the kitchen table and pulled open my textbook. I looked at the words written in the book, and the entire left side of every word danced in place. I couldn't read it because the left side was squiggling and wiggling. I closed my book and looked at the clock on the wall, but the numbers six through twelve twirled and swirled.

My chest tightened and my body sparked tiny jolts of electricity. "Jen!" I called to my roommate.

She came out of her room holding a can of Coke and a bag of gummy worms.

"Jen, I'm a little freaked out." The calm words hid my panic. "Everything looks really weird right now." My voice cracked as the fear broke through.

I called Student Health services on campus, left a message, and waited for the nurse to call me back. She sent us to the Emergency Department because "sudden visual impairment" could be serious. When I got into the Emergency Department and saw a nurse, the left half of my vision had quieted, and there was nothing to examine.

Even though my eyesight was fully functioning, I still had to see a doctor before they could discharge me. He told me that it was probably an ocular migraine, and the headache may or may not follow. That day, the headache

Chapter 1

never came. He told me to rest and relax and follow up with my doctor if the same visual disturbance occurred again. From that point forward, I never had another ocular migraine.

Feeling foolish for wasting her time, my time, and money, Jen and I trudged home with me lost in my thoughts as to if what I saw had really happened. Had I imagined the whole thing?

Fast forward fifteen years, and my migraines settled right in between my eyes. At its worst, it felt like a little man living inside my skull, and whacking the inside of my head with a tiny pickax. At its best, it was a constant dull ache that made me question my water consumption, amount of sleep, and level of exercise. No, I didn't have migraines every day, but I definitely had headaches every day.

"Besides," I said to Jessica, "I already saw my doctor for migraines, and she said it was nothing to worry about."

Jessica knew better than to press me for details when I downplayed my story. She changed the subject, and we talked about our kids. My two children were the bookends to her only child. My Alexandria was eight and Robbie was eleven, while her daughter, Malia, was nine. Even though Malia was technically older, she was in Alexandria's class. The two girls played softball together, had joined the same Girl Scout troop, and danced at the same studio. I often felt like Robbie was jealous of their immediate friendship, although he would never admit it. He was more of an introvert and would escape to his Lego building, science experiments, or video games every time Malia visited.

I had met Jessica when Alexandria was in preschool. She had just moved to Central Massachusetts, and I admired her ability to wear yoga pants and an oversize sweatshirt to preschool drop-off. I worked for a high-end marketing company outside of Boston and made sure I had at least one designer clothing item on display each day. I loved the work that I did, but I hated playing the game. I was tired of the pencil skirts and button-down tops, the matching jewelry and shiny watch. Not to mention, my three-inch heels that gave me blisters, so I would spent the evenings watching Jeopardy while soaking my feet in hot water and Epsom salt. In her comfy clothes and pulled-back hair, I saw Jessica and wished for an opportunity to step back, take a break, and be myself without any judging eyes.

After a week of admiring Jessica's lazy attire in the preschool parking lot, I decided to ask her out for coffee when I didn't have an early meeting scheduled. She wasn't the typical person I pulled to, but I couldn't take my eyes away from her laissez-faire attitude. Not only did it show in her clothing, but it showed in her beat-up Ford Explorer, her messy bun, and relaxed posture. I noticed that when myself and the other moms waited for the preschool doors to open, we stared at our phones, checked our emails, or watched random videos. We lived in a time when the days were short because work was long, and a society that expected maximizing and multi-tasking during all waking hours.

Jessica wasn't like that. That first week, I wondered if she even had a cell phone. She'd spent the mornings standing in line observing the others, almost like she was trying to figure out where she could possibly fit into this new lifestyle.

As an observer, she threatened to infringe upon the already established group of moms. She never spoke a word to anyone, just quietly watched.

By Friday morning, I got up enough nerve to say hello. "Your daughter is beautiful!" I said to the space between us.

Brought back to the insecurities of middle school, heat traveled from underneath my collar bone to my neck and my cheeks. The other mothers turned and glanced at me, not sure if I was talking to them, and I shot them a confident smile. Frozen and unsure how to get her attention without saying her name, I dropped my eyes and fiddled in my purse.

Mustering up bravery, I cleared my throat. "Excuse me," I said, walking directly into her line of vision. "My name is Ashley." I held out my hand and noticed the floppy handshake she returned. "This is my daughter, Alexandria," I pointed toward the little girl in the pink dress with matching bows in her hair sitting in the dirt and holding a rock. "Alex!" Flabbergasted, I walked away from the other mothers to wipe the dust off Alex's filthy dress. "Alex, get up, please. Your new dress is getting all dirty." I took the rock out of her hand and tossed it into the grass.

Chapter 1

Alex's eyes filled with tears and her little face crumbled. Quiet sobs escaped from her mouth and her shoulders shook. I reminded her that rocks were not toys, passed her the emergency snack bag I kept in my Kate Spade tote to distract her, and gave her a small hug. After Alex took a few bites of Goldfish, I dried her eyes and joined the new mom to continue our conversation.

"Jessica. That's my daughter over there. Her name is Malia," she pointed to the girl with the unkempt curly brown hair in the blue jeans. A canvas belt held up the excess fabric around the little girl's waist and the pant legs folded around her ankles. Her sock revealed itself behind the hole in the toe of her shoe.

"I haven't seen you before. Are you new to town?" I asked.

"Yeah, we moved here from New York. Not the city, but Upstate, near the Canadian border. I just got divorced, and Malia and I moved back home with my parents."

Ah. That explains so much. I looked at my newly manicured nails in Bubble Pop Pink and compared them to Jessica's stubby nails and calloused fingers. "Would you like to grab some coffee next week? I usually go into work late on Wednesdays."

Jessica smiled and nodded. "That'd be great."

I wasn't sure what made me invite her out or why she said yes. Perhaps it was how vastly different we were from the outside perspective. Her story intrigued me, and my parenting style probably intrigued her. I didn't have friends to speak of, and the idea of possibly gaining a friend outside of my work circle tempted me. Maybe someone so different could teach me something about relaxing and enjoying life. I knew I'd gotten grumpy since I married and had kids.

That first breakfast, Jessica was late. I was on a tight schedule and my annoyance grew with each passing minute. I sat in the booth at Marty's Diner holding a to-go cup of coffee and waited. She was fifteen minutes late. I decided to give her five more minutes, and if she still hadn't arrived, I would leave. I hadn't put myself in such a vulnerable situation in years. Disappointed at the prospect of being stood up, I tapped my fingers on the table and stared out the window.

With one minute to spare, a woman wearing a brown peacoat, a plaid scarf, and a newsboy cap entered the diner. She carried a large woven tote bag over her shoulder, and smiled with a wave.

"I am so sorry I'm late. My parents brought Malia to school, and I overslept," she explained, stripping her outerwear and dropping into the booth across from me.

"No problem." I waved my hand like I almost got stood up every day. "I noticed someone else dropped off Malia, so I wasn't sure if you were coming or not." I took a sip of coffee and looked up at her over the rim of my eyeglasses. "I have to leave in fifteen minutes," I added.

Jessica looked taken aback. "Oh, I'm sorry. Let me grab some coffee. We can talk for a few minutes. I have to get to the grocery store, so that's perfect. I'll miss the crowds." She smiled at me while waving down the waitress.

Even though our first date was a little awkward, I had found an instant coziness in her smile. She smiled at everything, as if little inconveniences in life didn't exist. As we talked, my shoulders relaxed and my body warmed with casual conversation.

I left Marty's Diner with another breakfast date scheduled on my calendar. Those weekly coffee dates kept me sane, reminded me to laugh, and taught me how to see life from another angle.

We had been doing those coffee dates for almost four years now. Those weekly outings turned into weekend family events, and eventually, my kids thought of Jessica as their aunt and Malia as their sister. Jessica and I learned to lean on each other for all significant life events: moves, boyfriends (hers, not mine), marriage (mine, not hers), kids, and school.

Over time, I showed Jessica more and more of myself. Between the dance recitals, art classes, and Girl Scout events, we shared moments, intimacies, and laughter.

She was my best friend, but I doubted I was her best friend. As the more open and approachable personality, other women trusted her and tolerated me hanging on the outskirts of their friendship. Her smile brightened the room, and she breathed reassurance. I knew that the way she made me feel was how she made everyone feel.

Chapter 1

Jessica worked at the kids school, and I learned about their classmates. I had my concerns about public education on a foundational level, and some of the stories she told made me think twice about sending my children. To ease my worried mind, she promised to keep an eye on my two as if they were her own.

School had started a few weeks back, and the kid's activities were in full swing.

My husband, Michael, was a custodian at the elementary school in the neighboring district. It worked perfectly because he was home with the kids after school, driving them to and from their activities, cooking dinner, and helping with homework. Whenever he had a free second, he would hide out in the garage making wooden doll furniture or painting beautiful canvases.

Most people called our family unconventional because Michael played the more prominent role in our children's daily lives, but it worked for us. I focused on work and making money, and he focused on keeping the family safe and happy.

Content with simplicity, Michael embraced his role. I found simplicity boring and predictable, and when things seemed too easy, I felt empty. Perhaps that was why I never left my job for motherhood. Being a parent overchallenged me because my children demanded every ounce of me. Being a parent didn't stimulate my mind the way learning and accomplishing goals did.

Michael happily woke at five, came home at three, and fell asleep by nine when the kids went to bed. I woke at five, got home at seven, and went to bed at eleven. Who needed sleep when you had coffee and wine? I learned to fully function on just a few hours of sleep a night.

I knew most women criticized me for putting my job first and my family second, but I viewed it as putting my family's happiness ahead of my own. I worked to live in a beautiful house with a flat, green yard, and a bathroom for every person. We traveled to extravagant locations every year to create memories that would last their lifetime. The kids danced and played softball during the year and went to technology camp every summer. I worked so that they would be happy. I tried not to compare myself to other women, which is why I never reached out to them on a personal level. If I ignored the stares and whispers, perhaps that meant that they weren't staring or whispering.

Jessica was the one person who never questioned my actions or decisions regarding motherhood. She had hit rock bottom right before we met, so she was in no condition to judge, and I found comfort in her. I needed a friend who needed me more than I needed her. Yes, I occasionally questioned my choices, but I would rather help solve her problems than admit that perhaps my orchestrated life wasn't as harmonic as I thought.

I thought about all these things as I looked out the window, watching the leaves dance on the sidewalk.

"Hey Jess," I said, grabbing her attention. "I'll keep a journal of symptoms. Maybe you're right. Not that I have a brain tumor, but maybe something else is going on. It could be anything, or it could be nothing."

We finished our weekly breakfast, and I headed to the office. I had a to-do list a mile long, and I knew it wouldn't get done if I didn't start. I opened the travel-sized pill bottle that I kept in my purse at all times, threw back two pills, and swallowed them dry. I wondered if someone could get addicted to over-the-counter headache medication, but I decided it didn't matter. I couldn't function without them.

Chapter 2

As fall arrived, the sun rose later and set earlier. I believed I was a farmer in a previous life. When the days became longer and sunnier during the spring and summer, I could go non-stop, with productivity filling every second of the day. When the clocks rolled back in the fall, my body struggled to adjust. Suddenly I couldn't wake up when I usually did, and driving home from work in the dark required extra attention.

I pulled out my therapy UV light and basked in the pseudo-sunlight for thirty minutes. The glow from the light lit up our office, despite the blackened windows from the night sky. I fell into this routine a few years prior when I realized my body's inability to function during the drab and dark winter mornings.

I had told my doctor how I struggled to stay awake during winter and my increasing difficulty getting up. My overall unhappy mood during the winter months followed me and I couldn't accomplish anything. He sent me to a psychologist who diagnosed me with general anxiety. He believed the transition into a new school year with my kids made everything more stressful, and suggested yoga and meditation to clear my mind. I didn't have time for that, so I shelved his suggestions, paid my co-pay, and went home.

"Do you think I have anxiety?" I asked Jessica over breakfast one Saturday morning. She looked at me with a slow grin spreading across her face.

"Yes. Do you?"

"Really?! I do not have anxiety! I mean, no more than anyone else, right?"

I knew that I had a lot going on with work, kids, and my husband, but I thought I was handling it like any other working woman.

"Ashley, what do you do after a stressful day at work?" she asked.

"Change into my pajamas and have a glass of wine," I replied.

"Okay, how long does it take for you to fall asleep at night?"

I hesitated, sensing where she was going. "Well, if I have wine before bed, maybe thirty minutes. If I don't have wine, maybe two hours or more."

"What exactly do you think about when you can't sleep?" she asked.

I made a face at her. She knew me too well. "I think about tomorrow. I run through the list of what needs to get done or what I need to remember. Am I ready for my work meeting? Is there anything important that the kids are doing that I have to ask about? Did I prep the coffee for the morning? What time do I have to get out of the house to spare myself maximum traffic? All sorts of stuff. And then, if it's something I can take care of then, I get out of bed and do it."

Jessica took a bite of chocolate pancakes. "There you go," she said between bites. "Anxiety. Do I think you're more anxious than others?" She shrugged and made a face. "I don't know. I think you care more than the normal person about having a clean house, clean kids, and keeping up with the image that you have your shit together, which I imagine creates more anxiety. I would say yes, you definitely do, but if you think you can manage it and manage it well, then you're fine. Don't let that psychologist get in your head."

"But Jess, why do you think winter is so much worse than summer? Can I have part-time anxiety?" I rubbed my hands on the chilly red vinyl of the seat.

"Maybe you have that seasonal thing, where you're affected by lack of sun. We do live in New England. In the summer, the sun sets after eight every night, and it sets at four in winter. At least in the summer, when you get out of work, you get some sunlight. We just turned back the clocks last week. Maybe it really affects you."

I thought about that seasonal thing after our breakfast. When I was in college, I applied to UMASS Amherst but didn't accept because the buildings

Chapter 2

didn't have enough windows. Everything looked drab and gray, and I couldn't picture myself enjoying that setting.

When I was a new mother, I struggled with the late-night winter feedings. It was cold and dark and too quiet. I often let Robbie cry until Michael couldn't take it anymore. He'd bring the baby to me to nurse in bed because I couldn't manage to pull myself from the warm covers. Michael did so much during that time. He helped Robbie every time he cried and would change him so that I would only have to do half the work. Michael told me it wasn't fair if I was the only one up just because he couldn't physically feed him.

Maybe Jess was right. Perhaps it was seasonal. I had researched Seasonal Affective Disorder and the symptoms of decreased Vitamin D. I bought myself a UV lamp because why not? It wouldn't hurt and could only help. Every morning during the fall and winter months, I woke up thirty minutes earlier to sit in front of that lamp glowing in my office. I used that time to catch up on the morning news and plan out my daily schedule, convincing myself it made a difference. It became part of my routine, and when I didn't use the lamp, I couldn't seem to get out of my own way.

I drank more coffee during the winter mornings and more wine during the winter nights. Looking back, I think I was compensating for winter depression. A light bulb went off in my head, and a sense of relief washed over me. It seemed the answer to all my problems had been solved.

I also noticed I exercised less, and gained more during the winter. For the past few years, I bought a new wardrobe before every season change. My clothes fit, but they didn't fit comfortably. A few pounds here, a few pounds there, it was just par for the course. I mean, you have Halloween (and honestly, don't all parents eat the kid's candy?), then Thanksgiving, then Christmas, and then New Year's. If you didn't pack on a few pounds, were you even human? My problem was that the pounds never left once spring hit and my exercise regime returned.

At every doctor's appointment for my yearly physical, I watched the scale slowly creep up. It bothered me, but I made excuses: I had stopped exercising; I didn't eat the healthiest; I bought lunch at work every day; My coffee and wine intake had increased.

I asked my doctor about it, and she shrugged her shoulders. She told me I was getting older (pushing forty did not feel old). Additional labs checked out year after year, and it seemed the scale added ten more pounds. I had to buy a new wardrobe in the next biggest size, and packed away the smaller clothes in case I could wear them in the future.

I talked to my husband about the weight gain because I never struggled with my weight before, and suddenly the extra pounds were sticking to me like glue. His response to my complaints was to pull me closer and tell me I was beautiful. I didn't believe him. Late at night, he would trace his fingers up and down my arm and kiss my shoulder. I would tell him I was tired and roll away from him.

I didn't feel happy, and I couldn't pinpoint why. I didn't believe it had anything to do with him, but my lack of energy and sexual desire affected our marriage. Night after night, I gave excuses: I'm tired; I have a headache; I have to get up early; I have a deadline. Before I knew it, we were having sex once a month. I felt like I had to, as part of my wifely duties.

I convinced myself that when summer came, things would be better.

The UV light dinged and automatically shut off. I climbed into the shower, got ready for the day, kissed everyone goodbye, and headed to work. The traffic was unbearable, but I made the daily sacrifice, so we could live in a large home with a good school district.

We moved to Central Massachusetts after I got my job in Boston. My parents died years ago, and Michael's parents were an hour away in Rhode Island. We realized that living in the suburbs of Boston was not an excellent fit for a young family. Our apartment was too small for the four of us, and carting a baby and groceries up and down three flights of stairs got old fast.

Throughout college and into our early years of marriage, Michael worked handyman jobs through word of mouth and mutual connections. He grew up under the guise of his carpenter father and learned how to build through observation. He didn't graduate from college, so he struggled with getting a "real" job.

We struggled financially during those years. We loved living in Boston and having the city at our fingertips, but we were too poor to experience any of it. It didn't make sense to stay in a place that suffocated us one rent check at a time, so we shoved our things into a small U-Haul and drove an hour west. I thought about that move, and although the commute from our new town to Boston was tough, it was the best thing we did for our family.

I quickly made a note on my phone: **2:30**.

I had to leave work early today because Alexandria had a Girl Scout meeting at four o'clock. I volunteered to be a scout leader a few years back, when the guilt of not being present in her life weighed on me like a ton of bricks. As a result, I had to leave work early once a month. I told my boss that I would work late the other four days of the week to ensure that everything I needed to finish got done.

With desperation in my voice, I had convinced Jess to be a co-leader since she worked with kids all day and knew how to handle the different personalities of children and parents. I dealt with the logistics, like the treasury and scheduling, and she dealt with the customer service, like the team building and behavior management. We made a good team, and I knew that if she hadn't helped, I would have quit a long time ago.

My drive home turned dark and blustery. It was only two-thirty in the afternoon, but the chill and the gray made it feel more like eight at night. The leaves swirled across the parking lot, and the clouds hinted at fat raindrops. I needed to pick up Alexandria and get to Jessica's house by four o'clock, cutting it close.

As I traveled down the Mass Pike, the gray clouds turn black. My headlights flickered on and I decelerated to avoid the potholes that quickly emerged. Tiny raindrops morphed into big, fat drops, and my wipers moved a supersonic speed. A sheet of water poured onto my car, and I squinted to make out the brake lights ahead.

My wipers swish-swish-swished at the fastest speed, and faint, blurred red lights illuminated against the bruised gray sky. Sitting forward and upright, I relied on my navigational skills instead of street signs. I crawled through the storm and eventually rays of sunshine bursted through the clouds.

Blinking my eyes a few times, I focused on the lights and signs ahead of me. I pulled off the exit and ran into the house to retrieve Alexandria. "Alex!"

I hollered up the stairs. "Come on, we're going to be late."

Michael stood in the kitchen loading the plates from the after school snack into the dishwasher. "Hey Ash," he said, eyeing me up and down. I walked over and quickly pecked him on the lips.

"Hi. I'm running late. We have our meeting at four-thirty, and we should be home by six. Maybe tonight we can watch a movie?" Again. The guilt of not being around motivated my actions.

"Sure, that would be great." I could see annoyance creep in Michael's eyes. He agreed to my invitation, but we both knew it wouldn't happen because something always came up. An email from work. A last-minute school problem. A forgotten homework assignment.

I grabbed a handful of Starburst from the candy bowl my grandmother gave me. The crystal cuts created prisms on the wall when the light hit it just right. "Alex, time to go," I hollered again.

My daughter tromped down the stairs wearing Converse sneakers and a black hoodie.

"Do you want a Starburst?" I asked, holding out my hand.

She sat on the stairs, tying her shoes. "Sure, can I have red?"

I handed her all the red Starbursts in my hand.

"Mom! I said red, not orange."

I looked at her blankly.

"I hate orange."

I took back the Starburst she called orange and brought them into the kitchen where the lighting was better.

"Hey, Michael? What color is this?" I asked, holding up the Starburst.

"Orange," he replied.

I continued to look at the small square in my hand. I grabbed the red Starburst that they called orange and the dark pink wrapped candy square. "What color is this?" I asked, holding up the dark pink.

"Red," Michael and Alex said in unison.

What? I placed both candies in the palm of my hand and walked over to the window. Then I walked directly below the kitchen light. I held up the two candies directly below the light and saw the colors transform. Red and orange, not red and pink. Pulling my hand away from the light, pink and red emerged.

"Hey, Michael? Do you think we can get some brighter lights? The shadows make it hard for me to see." I tried to hide the perplexity in my voice.

"Sure thing, beautiful. I'll replace them this weekend."

"Thank you." I rushed over and kissed him on the lips, said goodbye to Robbie, and passed the red Starburst to Alex. We hurried out the door and made it to Girl Scouts just in time.

Chapter 3

"Hey, Jessica, It's me, Ash," I said into the phone. "Call me when you can."

Breathing in the crisp November air, I walked around our neighborhood bundled up in a new scarf, matching hat, and black North Face jacket. I had just returned from the doctor's office again, and his lack of recommendations rolled through my head.

My complaint this time was about pins and needles in my chin.

I had been to my doctor for this same problem right after Robbie was born because my face frequently numbed late at night when I tried to sleep. My doctor, at that time, didn't find anything suspicious. It became another checked box in my medical chart. He referred me to a Neurologist "just to be sure," and when the neurologist said I was okay, I assumed it was all in my head. Probably stress and anxiety from having a new baby.

The tingliness never went away, though. Mostly it appeared late at night when I was trying to fall asleep. After a while, I accepted this weird sensation and decided that it was normal, and everyone probably felt it. But now, the tingliness was also in my chin. And sometimes in my fingertips. And other times in my toes.

Michael thought I was crazy, although he would never say that. I told him I would be home early from work today because I needed to see my doctor again. He usually listened to me complain, offered a vague and general

Chapter 3

explanation, and encouraged me to call the doctor. I had been to the doctor for more weird symptoms over the past few years than I could remember.

I went again, and this time I reviewed every strange, sudden, intermittent symptom I had experienced over the past few years. The weight gain, pins and needles, vision issues, headaches, and occasional dizziness that sprung up and disappeared like spurts of energy. He ran more lab work to check my thyroid and cholesterol, told me to track my food intake, and visit my eye doctor.

I always followed the rules, so I downloaded the food app and called my optometrist as soon as I left his office.

"Sorry, Mrs. Martin, but you had an eye exam seven months ago, so we are unable to see you unless you want to pay out of pocket." My heart pounded in my chest. I had the financial means to pay for another examination, but I didn't think I should have to.

"But you don't understand," I said, trying to convince her to change the rules. "I am having difficulty seeing."

"Well," the receptionist started, "the best we can do is check your lenses against your prescription. Perhaps there was a mistake when transferring the prescription to your glasses and contacts. You don't need an appointment for that, and it is free."

Deciding the exam would probably show nothing, I saved my two hundred dollars in examination fees for a rainy day. The majority of the time, I could see; it was sporadic when I couldn't. I was a maximizer and couldn't afford to take more time off of work, so I drove straight to the optometrist's office. He checked my lenses and told me they were correct.

"No problem there," the eye specialist said with a reassuring smile.

My thoughts jumbled together like a small tsunami, and I took my glasses back. Without saying thank you, I stumbled out of the store, convinced I was crazy. *Now what?*

I couldn't do anything until my labs returned, so I drove home to plan Thanksgiving dinner. Every year we hosted Michael's family for Thanksgiving, and this year the entire extended family was attending. I cooked a big turkey, and his sisters and parents brought over one dish or dessert. It was essentially a potluck, but I wrote the menu and delegated the dishes anyway.

Over the years, I learned who was good at making what and gently worked out the unpopular dishes, and replaced them with comparable sides that appealed to most guests.

Michael replaced all the lightbulbs with greater wattage so that I could see better. The kids complained that the lights blinded them, but I didn't notice. I tried to brush it off with old age. Wasn't that what everyone said? Your body changes every seven years? I saw all the essential doctors, and they said there was nothing concerning.

As I drove home, I noticed the sky transition to dark gray and the breeze pick up. The last thing I needed was to get caught in a rainstorm.

Walking into the empty house, I quickly got to work. I turned on all the lights in every room to get some extra light flowing into the office, and started on my list. Michael's mom, Janet, made an excellent stuffing. She usually was the first to arrive, so she could stuff the bird before it went into the oven. Janet and Michael's father, Hank, also brought the mashed potatoes and corn. Michael was raised in a family that stayed up late, woke up early, and ate meals two to three hours later than most Americans. Thanksgiving dinner was usually around seven-thirty at night, and I had adjusted to their schedule over the years.

When the kids were little, we went to Michael's parents' home in Rhode Island, and I despised the late dinner but would never say anything because it wasn't my family. My starving, cranky kids, and Michael and I, exhausted from chasing them around an unfamiliar house with fall hazards in every room, filled up on appetizers and snacks before the big meal.

After a few years of tolerating Thanksgiving at someone else's home, we convinced the family to come to our house and spend the weekend. I thought I could readjust the meal schedule, but I stood on an island, an early bird among a family of night owls.

All the women woke up at four am on Black Friday to go shopping. The thrill of getting a good deal consumed us all, and it became one of my favorite traditions with the Martin women.

Chapter 3

Michael's sister, Tiffany, brought the green bean casserole and glazed carrots, and his sister, Amanda, brought the pumpkin and apple pie. Amanda and her husband, Steve, had two children under three, so her pies had been store-bought the last few years. I let it slide because I knew she was overwhelmed with life. To be honest, the first five years of both of my children's lives were a complete blur. I remember moments but not the details, and I often confused which baby was involved with which event.

My older brother, Jason, came over for dinner with his wife, Melinda, and daughter, Ellie. She was eight, just like Alex, but the two girls barely knew each other. Jason and Melinda lived in New Jersey, which was just far enough to make it too far to visit. They stayed the weekend and we created a yearly tradition of buying their Christmas Tree at a local Christmas tree farm. They hauled it home on Saturday morning.

Without living parents or grandparents, it was just Jason and me for all the holidays. They brought a cheese and cracker platter and a vegetable platter for when we got hungry.

I wrote it down and studied the menu. It looked like enough food to feed the fourteen of us.

Mid-writing, my phone rang. "Hey, Jess."

"Hey, what are you doing at home? I saw your car in the driveway when I drove by. Is everyone okay?"

She knew that I was drawn to work like a moth drawn to a flame. It took incredible strength for me to pull away from my work. I knew I was good at my job, and not so great at being a mom or a wife. Returning to work started as an excuse to leave the house when I needed a break from the kids but it turned into my pride and accomplishment.

Well, until lately, when I couldn't keep things straight. Last week, I wore one blue and one black pump to work and then hid in my office because I didn't know how to explain myself. I assumed everyone at work was talking about me or thought I was losing it, so I kept myself busy behind my office door.

"I went to the doctor today."

"Oh, is everything okay?" she asked. I started to sense that my tales of potential illnesses were getting to her. I made a mental note to pull back on the play-by-play that I often gave her.

"Yeah, supposedly things are fine, but I'm still struggling with my eyes and experiencing all sorts of weird symptoms. Everyone says I'm fine, but I don't know. I just can't shake it."

I told her what the eye doctor said and how I needed to wait. Jessica told me to continue tracking my symptoms and take a break from obsessing and googling every possible ailment. She thought my anxiety could be triggering physical responses.

Lately, the million potential catastrophic illnesses I might have consumed my thoughts and distracted me from my life.

We cut our conversation short because Michael was due home any minute, and the kids would quickly follow. I needed to make sure I was emotionally available to them. When they came through the door, they were surprised to see me. Alex hugged me and asked for a snack, and Robbie dropped his backpack at the door and went to his room to play his guitar.

We cooked tacos for dinner, and I helped with homework. I briefly told Michael about my appointment. Instead of telling him how frustrated I was becoming and how most of the time my doctor's alluded to it all being in my head, I summarized I wouldn't know anything for a day or two until my lab results came back. I hoped he saw me as a competent, confident woman instead of the scared, anxious little girl I had morphed into when I was alone.

That night, Michael crawled into bed next to me and kissed me on the cheek. He looked into my eyes and said, "Ashley, I'm sorry you aren't feeling well. If something comes from it, I will be there for you. If nothing comes from it, I will still be there for you."

My heart swelled. I forgot how handsome he was and how caring his eyes were. I once admired the calloused fingers, creating ridges along the landscape of his hand. I loved how his messy brown hair felt against my fingers.

I gave him a deep kiss to communicate my love and desire. I wanted to continue with our intimate moment, but I feared nothing was happening down there.

Chapter 3

Ever since we had Alex, my body had stopped responding to Michael's touch. My head wanted to be intimate with him, but my body ultimately refused. I feared that we would get to that part of the experience, and Michael would roll over in a huff because my body would not cooperate. If my body didn't cooperate, did that indicate that my mind wasn't on the same page either? By not feeling aroused, did that mean that I wasn't in love with him anymore?

Terrified that the same course of events, the frustration, and my rejection of him would repeat itself, I willed my body to start responding. I didn't understand it, but I assumed the chaos of life and my age tricked my body into complete numbness.

It happened again. Nothing. He touched my nipples, and I couldn't feel anything. He kissed my neck, and I thought about Thanksgiving. It was another awkward moment of trying to jam a square into a circle. "Michael, this isn't working," I whispered with sad eyes. Placing my hand on his chest, I pushed him off me and rolled to my side.

"It's okay," he said as he stomped into the bathroom. I could feel his rejection when I saw his shoulders sag, and the fine lines around his mouth harden. I felt terrible, but I didn't know why. I knew I loved him. I knew he was the one, and I loved our life. Was this normal? Did this happen to every busy woman with kids who was approaching forty? This was the one area I didn't feel comfortable divulging to my doctor. My inability to be a woman embarrassed me and brought shame. Admitting a sexual problem indicated a bigger marital problem, didn't it? I feared counseling would open a door I didn't want to enter.

"I'm sorry," I called out to him as I hugged my body protectively. Michael didn't respond.

Chapter 4

"What was I doing again?" I asked for the hundredth time that day. Standing in the middle of my office, I scanned all the surfaces searching for something that would propel my next step. I looked around a second time, but nothing triggered my memory. I walked over to my desk and reviewed my to-do list. *Ah yes. The pitch for the new potato chip flavor.*

The printer jammed, my heart rate quickened and my palms seeped sweat. Only the first four pages stared back at me. *I need that report.* Like on a raft without a paddle, I pulled at levers and covers, rereading the help message on the copier, knowing if I didn't have that report for the meeting, we'd lose the account. The blurry, black words told me there was a paper jam but I couldn't find it. My chest tightened and I couldn't breathe. *Where was that paper jam?* In a last attempt I canceled the print job and restarted the copier.

"Ashley, are you ready?" My assistant Karen stuck her head into my office. "They're ready for you."

I quickly nodded and hit the Print icon on my computer for a second time. The pages spit out at a snail's pace. "I could do this faster if I hand wrote it myself," I grumbled under my breath.

I watched the seconds on the wall clock slowly tick away. Karen grabbed the printed document, threw it in a folder, and handed it to me.

"Thank you," I said and swallowed my nerves. Straightening out my suit

Chapter 4

coat, I walked into the conference room.

Four men and one woman greeted me. They surrounded one end of the large table, leaving the chair at the head of the table empty for me to fill it.

"Sorry I'm late," I said. "Just had a bit of printer trouble." I smiled at all the guests, hoping to communicate a go-with-the-flow, roll-off-your-shoulders kind of vibe. Their blank stares and flat lips reminded me this was no joking matter. Tension spread across my shoulders and down my back. I took off my suit coat, praying that sweat stains hadn't formed under my arms, and purposefully held my arms against my body.

Some of the advertising executives smiled back, and others sat stone-faced. Karen returned my smile, her eyes encouraging me to continue. I pushed my sleeves up, flashed my new watch, and fell into my presentation. I had practiced it in the car during my long commute, and knew the flow like the back of my hand.

Karen stood behind me, the PowerPoint clicker in her hand. I passed the document out to all and logged into my laptop, which already displayed my presentation. *Thank goodness for Karen.* I had forgotten to load up my presentation before I came into the room.

We whipped through the presentation, talking about the new ingredients, targeted demographic, and price. We discussed the motivation of the Millennial generation and why they wanted to make changes in the world. Gluten-free and vegan was the new "It" lifestyle, and we needed to jump on the train before it left the station.

To complete the presentation, I passed out chip samples arranged in a circle on the platter. Each colleague took a small bite and commented on the flavor, the crispness, and the texture.

Karen and I cleaned up the plates, thanked our guests, and exited the room.

"That seemed to go well," I said, smiling wide. I was good at my job. I loved to talk to people and convince them of what was great or why the competitor was not great, and I loved to sell. I was a true salesman at heart and knew how to spin things, so whatever I was advertising was something people needed.

"Yeah, too bad they tried Siracha instead of Bread and Butter," she laughed.

"Did you do that on purpose? To see who was paying attention?" My smile faded, and the color drained from my face.

"What do you mean? I put out Bread and Butter," I said. I tried to recall that moment when I pulled out the chips, but the memory blurred.

"No, you didn't. Did you taste it? It was NOT bread and butter. Maybe Siracha. It had spice." I grabbed a chip and smelled it. The spicy flavors seeped into my nostrils, and my stomach dropped in fear. I licked the chip. *Wait. How did that happen?*

"How did that happen?" The room tilted and I stumbled into my chair. "I opened the bag of Bread and Butter chips. I know I did. Siracha was the flavor our focus group decided was too strong. We weren't pitching Siracha. We were pitching Bread and Butter. I know I opened the Bread and Butter bag!" Panic strangled my voice, and the walls pressed down on me.

It wasn't just the chips; it was everything building up from the past few weeks. It was the missed appointments, the forgotten wallet, and the misplaced keys. It was the constant questioning of "What am I doing?" That question crept in at home, in the car, and now at the office.

"Ashley, it's okay," Karen soothed. "They liked it. I don't think they didn't even noticed. I wouldn't worry about it. The content is the same. It's just the flavor that was different."

I rummaged through the cabinet in the storage closet, looking for the chip samples given to the executives. A bag of Siracha and a bag of Bread and Butter sat side by side. Bread and Butter remained sealed shut, just as you would find it in a vending machine or at the grocery store. Siracha was open with a small chip clip on top. I stared at the bag, wondering how I made that monumental mistake. *Was I not paying attention? Did I not notice the scent?* I rubbed my forehead, feeling a headache coming on.

"You know what, Karen? I have a headache," I said, rubbing my thumb and forefinger over my eyebrows. "I'm going to take some Tylenol and finish up the Post-Meeting Summary. Please get me their feedback as soon as you can."

I slowly walked back to my office and sat at my desk. I couldn't concentrate after that mix-up, so I gulped a bottle of water, and closed my eyes for a

Chapter 4

moment. Between my brain fog and my headache, I struggled to focus on the computer screen before me. Even though I wasn't due to leave work for another two hours, I knew that I wouldn't get anything done if I stayed. I checked my calendar to see if I had any other meetings, grabbed my purse and keys, and left without telling anyone.

I somehow found myself in my driveway watching the sunset, feeling too exhausted to get out of the car. It was only four-forty in the early evening, and the sky was giving way to night. I looked toward the house and saw the shadows of Michael and the kids in the kitchen. They leaned over the kitchen table, possibly making pizza. I tried to recall the dinner menu I planned on Sunday night, but my brain couldn't recall the meals.

I couldn't see their faces, but could see their shapes move about, and I imagined that they were laughing and chatting about their day.

I felt like an intruder imposing upon the family routine that I was never a part of, although that was mainly my choice. My family wasn't expecting me two hours early, so they continued like normal, like I was at work.

I sat in the dark watching them through the brightly lit window. I watched them travel from the kitchen to the dining room table. I saw Alexandria clear their school work from the table, and Robbie set the table for dinner. Michael moved hot plates and dishes from the oven. I watched them sit together and share a meal, and my heart broke. I ached to be included and be a part of that moment, but I didn't want to interfere with the memories they were making.

The intensity behind my throbbing head had decreased, but I still struggled to see in the dark. I grabbed my purse and rummaged through the large tote bag looking for gum. I couldn't find it, and my movements quickened. Dumping the contents onto the passenger seat, I continued to search. *I know it's in here somewhere. I bought it this morning when I filled my gas tank. I had a slice of gum right after lunch. Maybe I left it on my desk.* My mind retraced my steps.

All I saw on the seat beside me were shadows of lipstick, Band-Aids, Chapstick, a hair tie, a pen, and a small notebook. No gum.

I grabbed my cell phone and turned on the flashlight app. Shining the light on the seat, the muted objects turned gray. I saw the perimeter of every object, but I couldn't differentiate what each thing was. It was like the outline of the objects blended into each other to create one heap.

My movements became more rigid and intentional as anger and disappointment grew because my eyes were failing me. And I messed up work, possibly costing us an account. *Why didn't my brain work anymore?*

Hot tears streamed down my face as I picked up every item and held it directly up to the flashlight beam. I tossed them into my purse one by one so I wouldn't confuse it with the mess left on my seat. Nestled under my phone, I found a small rectangle that resembled gum. I grabbed it and shined the light against it. *Double Mint. Finally!* Relief spread through me. Finding that gum proved I wasn't going crazy.

My body jumped like a Jack-in-the-Box to the rapping on the glass beside me. I turned to find Michael peering into the window with a big smile on his face. "Hey," he exclaimed. I quickly wiped away the tears that stained my cheeks.

"Hi, I came home early," I said with false enthusiasm, rolling down my window.

I didn't want him to think that I came home because I wasn't feeling well. I still had a headache but didn't think I had it in me to explain what I was feeling. I wanted him to believe that I had come home because I missed him and the kids. I wanted to be invited to their moment instead of barging in when they least expected it.

"Have you had dinner yet?" I asked, pretending I just pulled into the driveway.

"Yeah, actually, we just finished up. There's leftover pizza and salad if you're hungry." He opened my door to help me out of the high Range Rover seats. I grabbed my purse, put on my best smile for the kids, and entered the home we had built over the past eight years.

"Alex, Robbie, I'm home early today." I walked into the living room where both kids sat on the couch watching a rerun of Wheel of Fortune. I placed my keys in the basket and walked upstairs to change.

"Hey, Michael?" I called from our bedroom as I shimmied out of my black

Chapter 4

slacks and into a pair of sweatpants.

He poked his head into the room.

"Listen, I'm not feeling great, so I'm going to make a cup of tea and lay down. I hope you don't mind. It seems like the kids are relaxing, and I need to rest my eyes a bit. It's been a rough day."

Michael took care of me, like he always does. He carried a hot cup of tea into our room, and tucked me under the covers. "Do you need anything else?"

When I said no, he kissed me on the forehead and left the room. I didn't know how I had found such a perfect partner. The guilt weighed on me because I wasn't the perfect partner for him. It seemed I had changed over the last few years, and he deserved more than me. The guilt forever weighed me down.

The hot tea and cool compress on my head, combined with Tylenol, made me feel better. I couldn't keep my eyes open any longer, and I clicked off the bedside lamp, creating a darkness that was all too familiar. I didn't wake up until the following day.

My joints ached as I got out of bed, and I maneuvered into the bathroom. The sky shifted from night to day as I showered and brushed my teeth. My headache hadn't left me, and it traveled from in between my eyes to in between my ears along the base of my skull. I took the thermometer out of the vanity just to see if I had a fever. I needed to make sure I wasn't sick, as thoughts of the flu permeated my brain. The thermometer beeped and read 98.6. *Huh.*

I grabbed a washcloth and ran it under the cool water of the chrome faucet in our bathroom. My extremely outdated glasses sat on the shelf next to the double sink. I put them on and gazed at myself in the mirror, leaning forward to look at my eyes.

The right side of my face was crystal clear. The left side appeared fuzzy, almost like a painting. All the lines on the left side of my face blurred and muted. The right side of my face reflected bigger and closer than the left. I blinked a few times to see if my eyes still needed to wake up. No, my reflection continued to look like something you would see in a Funhouse mirror at the carnival.

"Michael?" I called out to him. *This is so weird.* I felt strange, like only one eye was working, and my head still hurt. "Michael?" I called again, racing into the kitchen where he waited for the coffee pot to fill. "Michael," I grabbed his arm. "Look at me." I moved his head with both hands, so his face appeared directly in front of me. The right side of his face was clear as day. The left side of his face blurred into a distorted blob. I looked at the clock on the microwave. It was seven-fifteen, and the vivid numbers one and five taunted me. I couldn't even see the number seven.

"Ash, are you okay?" Michael looked at me with a mixture of concern and confusion.

"I can't see," I blurted. *Maybe this was another ocular migraine. Perhaps it will pass, and things will be okay again.* I moved about the kitchen like I was searching for buried treasure, trying to keep myself busy while my jumbled thoughts stumbled over each other.

"What do you mean?" Michael asked with a smile.

I knew he thought I was overreacting. Over the years, we frequently discussed my hypochondria. Since we'd gotten married, I always sensed something was wrong with me. When I had a skin rash, I thought I had shingles. When I was dehydrated, I thought I had mono. When I sprained my ankle, I thought I had broken it. Google had become my best friend and my worst enemy. I constantly went to the doctor to hear that I was fine. The co-pays added up month after month and year after year.

I swallowed and took a deep breath to compose myself. "Michael, I am having a tough time seeing the left side of your face. I can only read the right side of the clock. I still have a headache. I think I might be having an ocular migraine." I sat down at the kitchen table and played with the sugar in the sugar bowl to keep my hands busy and my mind distracted.

"Ashley, you've been burnt out lately with work. Why don't you stay home today and rest? If it doesn't get better tomorrow, you can go to the doctor. Maybe they can draw some blood and do some labs. Maybe it's nothing."

I had a meeting today, but honestly, I had a terrible day yesterday. I wasn't overly excited to go in and see if anyone noticed that the chips they tried

Chapter 4

were from the wrong bag. I nodded to Michael. *Yes, maybe a day at home alone is precisely what I need.*

"You're right," I said, and I gave him a small kiss. "Here, let me help you with the lunches." I took the knife from his hand and proceeded to make peanut butter and jelly sandwiches for the kids. If I stayed home, I wanted to be an active parent. It was my responsibility to share the chores whenever I could. Making lunches was the least I could do before I slept on the couch all day.

I watched Michael in action, getting the kids ready for school and out of the house. It was impressive how he managed to juggle work and home with such ease.

After they left for the day, I lay in bed and didn't move until they returned. I spent the day analyzing my vision, looking at words in a book, pictures on the wall, various colors, and different lighting to see what made my vision clearer. Nothing made it better.

The next day I woke up and I could see again.

Chapter 5

The following day, I poured myself a cup of coffee and said good morning to Michael. He stood at the refrigerator, filling water bottles for the kids.

"Morning," he said without turning his head or pausing from what he was doing.

I walked over and gave him a quick kiss, half on the lips, half on the cheek, and told him I had to leave early to prepare for another meeting.

"Have a good day," he said with predictable eyes. Michael had always been patient with me in the past, but maybe he was tired of who I was becoming. Perhaps it wasn't just the lack of sex but also the uneven division of life responsibilities that weighed on him. Or my self-absorption and lack of involvement with our family. Whatever it was, I didn't want to talk about it, so I ignored his glance.

I walked away, trying not to take his nonchalance personally, and grabbed my bag. I kissed the kids and told them to have a good day. Robbie waved goodbye, and Alex reminded me that she was getting a Student of the Month award that afternoon. For the occasion, Michael had braided her hair, and she wore a new necklace with matching earrings. She wore her "coolest" flannel shirt, the one she wore to all special occasions. I congratulated her again and headed out the door without saying a word to Michael.

The drive into work was uneventful. I had driven this route for eight years,

Chapter 5

and could practically do it with my eyes closed. I knew exactly what time I had to leave the house to avoid traffic. My kids thought I was a drill sergeant about leaving and arriving on time, but I knew from experience if I left ten minutes too late, I would be sitting in traffic for an extra thirty minutes. Between construction and commuters, timing was everything.

I pulled into the parking garage at work and accidentally pulled too far. The underside of my bumper scraped against the concrete blocker. *Whoops! I guess I'm closer than I thought.*

Michael didn't believe I was a good driver. In fifteen years together, I had popped six tires, been rear-ended three times, crashed into his sister's car twice when backing up, and notoriously ran over curbs when taking a right turn. I guess he wasn't wrong, but at least I had never caused an accident.

I hurried out of my car to get into the office before everyone else. Today I had a meeting with Toy executives, pushing the next big Christmas gift.

Karen wasn't in yet, and I wasn't sure if she had prepped my presentation. I opened my computer and pulled out the file, peering at the PowerPoint slides. Some of the colors glowed brighter than the rest. I leaned closer to get a better look. Some of the text was blurry, but I didn't want to change it in case the new font was even worse on my eyes.

I didn't trust that my eyes would pull through for me in the big meeting, so I decided to ask Karen her opinion when she came in. Perhaps a blockier font or a larger size would look clearer.

I practiced out loud using the PowerPoint slides as a guide. I usually presented new material confidently in front of a group, but the font and brightness caused my anxiety to creep up. I found myself stumbling over words and struggling with organizing my thoughts. The environment around me tilted, so I closed my eyes to reset my mind. I kept them closed and tried to recite the talking points, but my equilibrium swayed and the blackness behind my eyes spun like the ballerina in my daughter's music box. The darkness behind my eyes tilted and wobbled. I snapped my eyes open, reorienting myself to the light, and paced around my office while speaking out loud and emphasizing keywords.

Karen came in, and I asked her about the font and the brightness. She told me this was the format we used every time. I brushed her response away and pretended that my question was typical. Based on her quizzical expression, I knew she thought I was crazy.

We headed to the conference room to find six executives sitting upright with laptops in front of them. I stood at the head of the table and looked around. We carried multiple accounts with this client, so I knew all the people in the room on a professional level.

I looked around to smile and greet them, but I couldn't see their faces and I didn't know who was who. All I could identify was hair color, clothing color, and if the person was male or female, yet I was less than ten feet away. My heart rate increased, my face flushed, and my palms got sweaty. I wasn't nervous about the pitch; I was nervous because I had to pitch a product to a group of people I couldn't see.

I refused to let this stop me. My voice cracked and wavered throughout the presentation. I tried to make eye contact but declined to address anyone by name because I didn't know who was sitting where. I couldn't gauge their facial expression and had no idea if they liked it or hated it. Continuing like a steam train accelerating down a hill, I rumbled toward the station, picking up steady speed. I was out of control, so consumed with my panic, I didn't know what words were leaving my mouth.

My brain was not in the meeting. Am *I dying? Is something seriously wrong?*

I think Karen identified the stress on my face and sensed that I wasn't on my A-game. She stepped in, fielding questions and going back to pertinent slides to support her answers. She took over the meeting and I stood behind her, smiling like a statue, begging my brain to start working.

When the meeting was over, I shook hands, getting up close to their faces. My body relaxed, realizing I could see who was who if I got close enough.

I rushed back to my office with Karen trailing behind me. "Ashley, are you okay?" she asked. "You look pale."

"I'm not feeling well," I responded. "I think I need to call the doctor."

Karen hesitated at my open door and tiptoed away. I locked the door behind her and fell into my chair behind my desk, bawling lonely tears into my hands.

Chapter 5

Embarrassed by how the pitch went, I berated myself for not keeping it together. Again. I wouldn't be surprised if I ended up getting fired for all these stupid mistakes that made me look incompetent. I couldn't understand what was wrong with me, and fear emerged deep within my core.

I called my doctor to see if my lab results were back. The nurse told me that everything checked out in the normal range. Not surprised but also astonished, the symptoms rolled through my head like a loop.

I called my eye doctor, begging him to see me. The receptionist put me on hold, and when she came back, she said, "Dr. Patel is not able to see you unless you pay out of pocket." Then she whispered, "I'm not a doctor, but I used to work for an ophthalmologist, and based on what you're saying, I think you need to see them, not us. I don't want to scare you, but there could be something seriously wrong with your eyes. I saw a lot of people come in with eye issues like what you are saying. There is a clinic at the hospital you can try. It's a walk-in. You might be waiting for a while, but at least you will get seen." Then her voice raised to an average volume, and she continued, "Would you like to come in and see the doctor?"

I thanked her for her help and quickly hung up the phone.

I emailed my staff explaining that I had to leave suddenly for a family emergency and would be back tomorrow. I couldn't tell anyone at work what was going on because I didn't know anything, and I didn't want to jeopardize my job. Karen knew something was wrong, but she didn't have enough information to start any rumors.

I knew I shouldn't have driven, but I did. It was a walk-in clinic that also scheduled appointments, so I added my name to the walk-in list and hoped there weren't many people before me.

While waiting, I texted Michael to tell him where I was in case something happened. I knew he wouldn't get the text until lunchtime, and I hoped the nurse would call my name by then. I watched people come and go. Every time someone wearing scrubs walked into the room, my heart stopped, waiting in anticipation. Finally, after four hours, I heard someone say, "A. Martin?"

Dr. Ling, the ophthalmologist, brought me into his office to get a detailed history of my symptoms. I gave him everything: my blurry vision, dizziness, Seasonal Affective Disorder, fatigue, headaches, weight gain, pins and needles, and most recently, not seeing details in objects. His assistant brought me into a room to complete the assessment.

During the acuity test, the severity of my symptoms hit me. I had my glasses on, and I could only read the top two lines. Everything else was entirely blurry or missing. I knew I failed and fear rose from my chest up to my throat. I swallowed the rock sitting in my neck and told the assistant that I could not decipher any other letters. Quiet tears streamed down my cheeks.

She brought me over to a machine and explained that they would take pictures of my optic nerve. Then she showed me a booklet with numbers in it and asked me to read the numbers. The numbers changed depending on where I looked. If I looked in the middle of the number, I saw a seven. If I looked to the left of the number, I saw a 2. It happened time after time, and I knew I failed that test too. I closed my eyes, fighting back the tears. *What was wrong with me?*

Next, Dr. Ling held up a marker and asked me to label the color with one eye closed. My right eye saw red. My left eye saw orange. He jotted down notes in his computer, keeping a straight face. I sat there quietly, digesting all that I learned. *I can't see letters, I can't see colors, and I can't see numbers. I knew there was something wrong, and everyone had brushed me aside time and time again.* Anger toward the medical field poked at my skin, and I bit down on my lip. Tears filled behind my slit eyes and I shook my head at the reality of my situation.

Dr. Ling pulled his chair right over to me. "You have Optic Neuritis," he said, "which is inflammation of the optic nerve."

I nodded like I understood, but I didn't.

"I believe you have had it for a long time based on the presentation of your optic nerve. How long have you been noticing these symptoms?" he asked.

"Years," I responded. "I've noticed symptoms on and off since my youngest was born eight years ago, but the vision stuff started to affect me a few months ago."

Chapter 5

"What did the vision stuff look like a few months ago?"

"Um." I tried to remember and I scrunched my forehead. "It was like I was wearing sunglasses all the time. It didn't matter if I was inside or outside, or if the weather was rainy or sunny. No matter where I was, everything was dark, like I was wearing sunglasses."

"Interesting," Dr. Ling said. "Well, you must make an appointment with a neurologist and get an MRI done of your brain. As soon as possible. Based on what I am seeing, it looks like you have Multiple Sclerosis, and it appears you have had it for quite some time."

I stared at him, not quite understanding. *Multiple Sclerosis?* I didn't know much about that disease, but I did know that it was lifelong, progressive, and debilitating. I had a few family members who had it, but I didn't know many details about their journey with the illness.

Unable to quiet my busy mind, I gathered my stuff and made my way to my car. I drove home, terrified that I would crash, but my anger toward my potential diagnosis flew me home in a blur. I wanted to cry, and I could feel the tears building, but I couldn't allow myself to go there because my sight would be further compromised. The sky had darkened. The last thing I needed was to miss my exit because the tears blocked my vision further.

When I arrived home, the entire family was there. Again, Michael asked why I was home so early. He hadn't received my text because his phone died.

"I went to the doctor," I said.

He raised his eyebrows at me. "Again?"

"I'll talk to you later," I said. I couldn't pretend any longer. My body moved on autopilot, and I felt like a zombie.

That evening I kept myself busy helping with dinner, homework, and chores. I needed to stay active because I wasn't ready to address the elephant in the room, and I certainly wasn't prepared to talk to my children about it. Before I told my kids, I needed to know the facts to answer their questions.

I stayed up late that night googling Multiple Sclerosis. *Fatigue-check. Numbness and tingling-check. Vision problems-check. Dizziness-check. Sexual problems-check. Cognitive changes-check.*

I didn't have all the symptoms, but I certainly had many. I searched for treatment options and personal stories. I could not believe this was real.

That night in bed, Michael listened to me rehash my day. I told him how scared I was at work and how devastated I was at the doctor's office. I told him how I waited hours to get an answer. It seemed I could have Multiple Sclerosis, and I was terrified. I cried into his shoulder because the weight of the suspected diagnosis was too much.

What I didn't tell him was how sorry I felt for being a disappointing wife. Or sorry I was never home to share the household chores. Or too tired to spend time with him. I couldn't tell him that I felt like a shell of a person, teetering on a mental breakdown. Or that I felt like a failure all the time.

I sat in our king-sized bed with the satin sheets and fluffy down comforter, holding a half-full glass of wine in my clammy hand. I had the life I always dreamed about, and it was completely falling apart.

Michael reminded me gently that I didn't have a diagnosis yet, and it wasn't a life sentence. He told me that no matter what was determined, he would be there for me.

We decided that we wouldn't tell the kids until we knew what was happening.

Chapter 6

The next day, Michael and I stayed home from work. Overwhelmed with my almost diagnosis and up all night "researching" my possible disease, I hadn't slept a wink. Multiple Sclerosis searches had turned to hospital websites, and then personal blogs of people living with the illness. It was too much.

Before we got the kids to school, I dodged questions I wasn't ready to answer. Alex asked why I was home all the time, and I told her I needed to see more doctors. She accepted my answer and didn't push further. Robbie didn't seem to notice the change in atmosphere or the increase in tension within our home.

There was a thick cloud of melancholy permeating into all the rooms while I sipped my coffee in silence.

"Michael, should I call the doctor about scheduling an MRI? I just saw him," I said.

He stumbled around the house, picking up the breakfast dishes the kids had left on the table. "Yeah, you need to get a referral from him."

Dying to get out of my prickly skin, I turned on the news until the office opened. The nurse said she would put a referral in, and someone would call in a few days.

Waiting was torturous.

After that eye appointment, when I failed everything, I decided that driving was unsafe until they gave me a diagnosis and treatment plan. I didn't go to work for the rest of the week because my eyesight was not good. I told myself I could work from home if needed, but I couldn't concentrate.

I talked to my manager and told him that I had a medical family emergency happening, and I would be taking my Paid-Time-Off for the rest of the week. I decided to deal with Monday when Monday came.

Michael also took off work to keep me company. I believed his motivation was to figure out if what I was experiencing was real. He always supported me, but he also always joked that I had to have something wrong with me at all times. He stayed with me those two days while we waited in anticipation for the neurologist to call. We talked about what I saw and what I didn't see. It wasn't improving.

On Friday, Dr. Smith called and scheduled my Neurology appointment for December fifteenth. My eyes widened, and I asked if there was any other appointment sooner, even with a different doctor in a different practice. I begged him to find some opening in the calendar. I couldn't wait another thirty days, not knowing what was wrong with me or how to fix it. He told me that with the holiday season approaching, availability was limited.

My lips curled and I cracked my knuckles, stomping my feet as I entered the kitchen. I imagined doctors and nurses laughing and joking around the Thanksgiving table while I tried to entertain blindly.

Swallowing my animosity, I thanked him for his time. It wasn't his fault he was the messenger.

I called the Neurology office and again asked if there was anything sooner. The kind receptionist told me she would put me on the cancellation list. Next on my list was Dr. Ling, where I left a message with his nurse. I needed to know if there was anything I could do that would improve my vision enough to drive. Dr. Ling called back and suggested steroids to reduce the inflammation, but I needed to see a neurologist first.

Exhausted, hopeless, and helpless, I sat in my bed and slept.

***

The following Saturday morning, I sat across the table with Jessica, eating my strawberry pancakes with a side of sausage. This dessert breakfast was

Chapter 6

one of my favorites, but today it tasted like cardboard. The strawberries looked brown.

Besides a few text messages asking about Girl Scouts and PTO fundraisers, I hadn't spoken to Jessica in a week. I was afraid to talk about my latest news because I would cry if I spoke about it. Instead, I stuck my head in the sand like an ostrich, and focused on her.

It required all my effort to hold myself together and I refused to fall apart in front of my kids. Without any answers, I didn't even know what questions to ask. I refused to lie to my children, so I said nothing and allowed my silent tears to run down the drain in the hot shower.

Jessica knew something was wrong because I had asked her to pick me up. I lied and told her my car was in the shop, but she might have seen the top of my SUV poking through the garage door windows. She allowed me to push food around my plate, watching me, waiting for the perfect opportunity to wedge herself into my current dilemma.

"How are you feeling?" Jessica asked, stirring her yogurt parfait.

"I'm okay," I replied. I couldn't meet her eye.

"How have your headaches been lately?" She poked with compassion and waited for an answer. I looked at her face but could only make out one eye.

"They're okay," I lied again. I felt alone and vulnerable. I was supposed to be the strong one, the one who knew what to do in every situation. I was the one who held it all together. These feelings made me uncomfortable within my skin.

"You look like you haven't slept in days," she said, point blank.

"I haven't." My voice cracked. My inner voice beat myself up for showing weakness.

"What's going on?" Her words wrapped tenderness and comfort around me. I knew this was her teacher voice when her five-year-old "kids" came to her with a scraped knee from recess or a forgotten lunch at home.

I couldn't stop myself. The words tumbled out about my journey with my primary care, to the receptionist at the optometrist's office, and then to Dr. Ling. My suspected diagnosis, the Neurology appointment that was never going to come, and my frustration with the medical system as a whole fell out of my mouth in a lengthy monologue. My eyes filled with tears from feeling out of control, but I demanded that they not fall, and they didn't.

"Ashley, what are you going to do? You can't stay home for a month!" Those were my sentiments exactly. I shrugged my shoulders, unable to speak. I would call on Monday and explain my situation to see what my options were. I had been there long enough and proved myself time and time again. I didn't think they would ostracize me or replace me. Even if they wanted to replace me, I didn't think they could without a legal battle.

"I have confidence in Karen and her ability to keep our office afloat."

There wasn't much to discuss regarding my new medical problems, so the conversation quickly transitioned to kids and work.

It was nice seeing Jessica and sharing the confusion surrounding me. I hugged her goodbye and told her I would text her later. All I wanted to do was sleep until December fifteenth, when I could get on a treatment plan to make my symptoms disappear.

That night Jessica called me with urgency in her voice. "Ashley, remember a few weeks ago when I told you that you might have a brain tumor? You might have a brain tumor." She spoke with an urgency in her voice and my attention turned to our current conversation.

I stepped outside onto our deck, overlooking the woods. "What are you talking about? The doctor thinks I have MS," I repeated slowly.

"I hope you don't mind, but I called my sister Allison, in California, and she said that without a brain scan, they can't say for certain that you have Multiple Sclerosis." Allison was a nurse and lived in Los Angeles. She worked on a neuro floor and saw various things from Traumatic Brain Injuries to strokes to Parkinson's. "She said sometimes brain tumors act similarly to Multiple Sclerosis and that if you have a tumor on your eyes, it could cause blindness. Ashley, you can't wait another month to see a doctor. That is crazy." Jessica pressed.

My hands started to sweat, and I gripped the phone closer to my ear. I lowered my voice so no one could hear me. "But what can I do? I already called the doctor. Obviously, if they were worried, they would have gotten me in sooner."

Chapter 6

"You have to go to the ER. That is the only way you will get an MRI immediately. Obviously, you can't go in there and demand an MRI, but they will figure it out if you go in and talk about all your symptoms. She said you have to go to Boston because the local hospitals around here aren't experts in MS or brain tumors. Boston has the best hospitals."

I rolled my eyes, but she couldn't see me. I was not going to Boston. It was far enough away to be a hassle. I imagined the wait in the Emergency Department was forever long. "I can't," I said. "Robbie has his building competition tomorrow, and the Girl Scouts are volunteering at the Apple Tree Nursing Home on Sunday. I can't miss it. I already miss enough of their lives." There was silence on the other end. "Jess? You there?"

"Yeah, I am here. I'm thinking. You aren't going to work on Monday, right?" she asked.

"No, I don't feel safe driving," I responded.

"Okay. Kids get on the bus, and we go to Boston. We'll get to the ER around ten after the traffic lets up. Maybe we'll wait a few hours to get seen, and then we'll be on our way home by six. Do you think Michael could watch Malia until we get home?"

My brain couldn't process the information. Jessica was going too fast. *The hospital? I hated hospitals. Boston. Brain tumor.* The reality of my situation dug its claws into me, and I felt my lungs deflate.

Struggling to breathe or think, I rubbed my forehead. "Um…" That damn headache was back, and this time my eyeball was throbbing too. "I'll talk to Michael and call you back."

"Please, Ashley," Jessica begged. "You can't wait until December." I knew she was right, but I still didn't want to go to the hospital.

Michael agreed that waiting until December was too long. He agreed to watch Malia after school until we got home. I didn't want to share what Allison had said because I didn't want to worry him until we had more information. Plus, I wanted to enjoy my weekend.

Afraid I'd disappoint the kids or concern them with my worries, I planned on going to Robbie's technology competition on Saturday and the Girl Scout trip on Sunday like nothing was out of the ordinary.

Robbie joined a Technology program earlier in the year through his science class. It pulled him from recess once a week to work on a Lego project, and he talked about it often. Most kids would be opposed to missing recess consistently, but Robbie came home that first week of school waving the sign-up sheet, asking if we would sign him up. His favorite teacher was teaching the group, and his best friend Sam signed up as well.

Robbie and Sam created a spacecraft from scratch using specific Lego blocks for the building competition. As the competition got closer, he came home from school, sharing their design and how it was coming together.

I knew how proud he was of his creation and what a big deal this was, so I put on an enthused face and pretended there was nothing wrong.

The gymnasium where the competition took place was full of people milling around. Some walked with long strides, running around the gymnasium to put out fires, while the kids added last minutes details before judging occurred. The kids stood with grins across their faces, beaming with pride as their friends and family congratulated their efforts.

From my perspective, all the people and all the colors blended into each other. I felt like I was living in an acrylic painting.

I didn't have a headache today, but I felt disoriented with all the sensory stimuli crashing through my brain. The noise, colors, movement, and crowd made me anxious, and the familiar pull of my chest tightening increased. The room slanted from side to side, so I sat down next to Robbie and Sam as they tried to perfect their build before the judges appeared.

"Robbie, this is amazing." I looked at his spacecraft without really seeing the details. From where I was sitting, it looked like a giant triangle. "Do you mind if I sit here for a few minutes?" I asked.

Michael and Alex roamed around the gymnasium, looking at the competition, but I couldn't find them in the blur of the crowd.

"Sure, Mom." He turned his attention away from me and greeted the person approaching. "Mr. Carter, hi!" Robbie waved, and I recognized his teacher's name and smiled in his general direction.

Mr. Carter approached the table with the school principal, Mrs. Schwartz. They checked the tables to make sure we were ready for judging.

Chapter 6

Mrs. Schwartz wore a black and white striped dress with thin, horizontal stripes. I looked at her dress, and suddenly the lines started moving up and down and side to side. I closed my eyes to reset them and looked back at her. The lines continued to move, and the background of the gymnasium tilted. Suddenly I felt like I was hungover, and the room spun in slow circles. As quickly as it started, the spinning stopped.

I closed my eyes for a moment, wondering what the heck was wrong with me. Hotness invaded my body, and I couldn't breathe. I interrupted Robbie and Sam's presentation and ran outside. The chilly hair hit me like a wall, and I collapsed on the sidewalk, my legs stretched into the parking lot. I didn't care that my Donna Karan pants got dusty or that the frostiness of the concrete seeped through my chilled bones. I didn't care that I had left my jacket inside. I stayed there, stuck on the sidewalk, looking around my surroundings, trying to figure out what was triggering my eyes to go haywire.

I made my way into the gymnasium just in time for the awards ceremony. Parents and community members filled the bleachers. The judges sat on a podium in the middle of the gymnasium, and the contestants' tables sat behind them. I scanned the audience, looking for my family, but I couldn't make out their faces. After a few moments of searching, I resigned myself to the seat closest to the door.

"Everyone did an amazing job today!" Mr. Carter said into the booming microphone. "We have had the honor of watching the kids grow in creativity and building and are excited to announce our Blue-Ribbon Builders!"

Suddenly the gymnasium filled with thunder as the kids drumrolled on their tables, being ever so careful not to knock over their builds.

"Sam and Robbie, please come to the stage!"

I couldn't believe they won. I straightened my back to get a better look and clapped. Proud of all work, I rose to my feet and continued clapping. The two boys took their ribbons and bowed before the audience.

After the competition, we went to Robbie's favorite restaurant for dinner. "Why didn't you sit with us?" Michael asked as the waiter put down our drinks.

"Oh, I didn't know if there was room," I lied. "And I didn't want to block people's view of the kids." Michael gave me a look that told me he didn't believe a word I said but would not press for more information.

I struggled reading the menu but knew I could order a salad or a sandwich. Our waitress came over, and I ordered a tossed salad with house dressing. I wasn't hungry. I just wanted to go home and rest.

After dinner, we went home, and I rummaged through the cabinet for Tylenol. I wasn't sure if Tylenol would help, but I thought it was worth a shot. I sat on the couch and fell asleep while the rest of the family watched a movie. My kids didn't question my behavior today, so I continued to pretend everything was fine.

I couldn't wait to get to the hospital Monday morning.

Chapter 7

"What's going on today?" the intake nurse asked while facing her computer and typing on the keyboard. Jessica sat outside the room, waiting for me to get the okay to enter the Emergency Department.

"Well, I have been struggling with my eyes lately," I responded.

"How long has it been happening?" she asked.

"Oh, I don't know. A couple of weeks," I replied.

"If it is a chronic problem, I don't know if the Emergency room doctors can help. It sounds to me like this is something you should see your doctor about instead," she answered, still looking at her computer screen.

"Well, it's gotten exponentially worse within the past few days," I responded, ignoring her snarky comment. *How dare she make me feel like I am wasting their time. I'm going to get to the bottom of this today.* "And I've been having horrendous headaches."

She gave me my wristband and told me to wait in the first waiting room. We arrived before lunch, just as planned. There were only four parties in the waiting room with us. Forty-five minutes later, we entered a room with an examining bed. I explained my symptoms to the nurse, then a doctor, and then a neurologist. The doctor came back in and said that they would be doing an MRI of my spine, neck, head, and eyes because, based on my report and the notes from Dr. Ling, it appeared that I might be suffering from Multiple Sclerosis. Again, that word.

We waited in another waiting room full of sick people. Nurses moved to various patients sitting in the waiting room, some wearing regular clothes, some wearing pajamas, and some wearing hospital gowns. It was evident there weren't enough beds available for all the people in need.

Patients filled the room like sardines in a tin can, and I tried to sit as far away as possible. There was a sign on the wall that said the MRI wait time was three to five hours. I stared at the television in the far corner of the wall, unable to see or hear it.

Jessica tried to keep my mind off things by chatting about anything and everything. She went to the cafeteria and brought back lunch. We ate together, looked at magazines together, and tried to watch TV, but the news only distracted me so much. We sat in silence, lost in thought about what might happen next. I felt comfortable with her there next to me. *If Michael couldn't be here, Jessica is the next best thing.*

Hours later, the nurse finally called me in for an MRI. I had no idea what to expect because I had never had one before. They put me in a wheelchair and wheeled me down a maze of long corridors. We arrived at a room with a big warning sign above the door due to the incredible magnet that could rip metal off your body.

I signed a waiver, but I didn't read it. I just wanted it done.

I lay on the narrow plastic plank and placed my head on the cushion. The technician placed a warm blanket over my legs and told me it would take close to two hours. They told me to stay still, and placed earplugs in my ears and a helmet over my head. I closed my eyes and held a squeeze ball just in case I had to get out of there.

Boom-boom-boom-boom! Chicka-chicka-chicka-chicka-boom-boom-boom! The noise inside the tunnel vibrated through my body. Swallowing was difficult because I couldn't move my head. My arms fell asleep, and my fingers turned to ice.

I focused on breathing and counted to ten over and over to pass the time. Every time a new series of bangs and booms happened, the technician told me how long it would last. When she told me three minutes, I tried to count

Chapter 7

the entire one hundred and eighty seconds. The back of my mouth filled with saliva, and I focused on not swallowing until the bangs stopped.

In my mind's eye, I sat in a hot bathtub relaxing with soft music and a good book. I pictured myself driving through the countryside in our convertible. I imagined myself on the beach sipping a Margarita. I focused on the things that brought me pleasure and ignored the rising need to panic.

A loud voice interrupted my thoughts. "Okay, we finished the initial scans. We are sending them to the doctor to see if we need more."

I continued to close my eyes, afraid that if I opened them and processed how small the tube was, my body would cave in on itself in paranoia.

After a few moments, she said, "We need to do one more scan. There will be three more pictures." I continued to practice my relaxation techniques, knowing that I only had to get through ten more minutes.

After that, I returned to the waiting room. The nurse who took my blood pressure when I arrived told me someone would be with me soon.

I looked around at all the sick people, wondering about their ailments. The nurse came over to the patient next to me, and I continued to stare at the television, trying my hardest not to eavesdrop. Still, the words "diarrhea" and "gastrointestinal" invaded my consciousness. My body shifted to the far end of the seat, trying not to breathe the same air. I could not wait to get out of there. It felt like I had been there all day with no hope of leaving, and I knew too much medically about all the strangers closest to me.

Jessica and I found the bathroom, and when we returned to the waiting room, we sat in the opposite corner of the woman with the stomach bug. Anxiety melted off my shoulders, but I had no idea what type of ailment I was sitting next to now.

"Thank you," Jessica mouthed to me.

A small woman with straight, dark hair, a petite frame, and round glasses came to me with my nurse. "Hi, Ashley? My name is Dr. Saunders. Can you come with me, please?"

I blindly followed her, with Jessica trailing behind. My heart thumped out of my chest as I entered the room, and she closed the curtain. "We have your MRI results back, and I have some good news and some bad news. What would you like first?"

I looked at Jessica, and she had her notebook opened with pen poised in hand. She knew that I wouldn't remember anything the doctor said or understand its meaning, so she was ready to take notes and be an extra set of ears. "The good news," I requested.

"Well, the good news is that we thought you might have Multiple Sclerosis, but there is no sign of demyelination on your spine or brain."

Relief flooded through me, but fear slowly crept back. "If it isn't Multiple Sclerosis, what could it be?"

"Well, that is the bad news. We found a growth along the base of your brain, and it is sitting on the optic chiasm, which is where the two optic nerves cross. It is mostly on the right side. We don't know for sure, but we think it might be a pituitary macroadenoma. It is about 3 centimeters by 3 centimeters, so it is rather large."

I stared at her blankly. *A what?* Jessica furiously wrote down everything, often asking the doctor to repeat or spell the medical terms.

"We need to admit you. You'll be meeting with the neurosurgeon and other specialists during your stay to determine the next steps." She told me she didn't have any other information and escorted us back to the waiting room.

I told Jessica I needed a few minutes to call Michael, and I sneaked back into the empty room where we first heard the bad news. I didn't bother to shut the curtain and sat on the examination bed, with fingers shaking.

"Hi Michael," I said, trying to sound as normal as possible. My protective instinct kicked in, and I wanted to soften the blow. I could hear the kids in the background chatting noisily. "So, I just heard back from the doctor, and I don't have MS," I said with forced enthusiasm.

"Oh, that's great," he said.

I closed my eyes, not quite knowing how to break the news. "Now, I don't want you to panic," I started, "but they did find a tumor, and it's sitting on my optic nerve. That's all I know. I am being admitted tonight." *There you go. Rip the band-aid off quickly.*

There was silence on the other end. I wasn't sure if the call had dropped. "Michael? Are you there?" I asked. "Can you hear me?"

Chapter 7

"Yeah," his voice sounded hollow. "Are you okay? What do you need me to do?" I heard his voice catch in his throat and I pulled my broken pieces together.

I told him I needed him to not panic and to keep the kids calm. I needed him to wait patiently until I had more information. Jessica would pick up Malia before eight. Just like at work, I delegated tasks in a predictable fashion. Always matter-of-fact and to the point.

After we hung up the phone, I sat on the bed in the empty room and cried hot, angry tears. I still didn't understand what was happening, but I could tell by the young doctor's face that it wasn't good. I wiped my tears and walked back to the Emergency waiting room.

"You should go," I said to Jessica. "Michael's expecting you around eight."

It was now almost five.

"But traffic," she said.

"I'll be fine," I said. "I'll text you later." I gave her a hug and watched her leave. My heart broke at the thought of being alone during this unknown time, but I had to remain strong.

I emailed work and told them I wouldn't be in for the next few days, and prayed to God to protect my family no matter what the path looked like until this journey ended.

A variety of doctors, nurses, and fellows questioned me while I waited for a room to become available. I told my story on repeat, each version shortened than the last. None of the doctors gave me any information about the severity of my condition or what the next few days would look like. They all smiled at the end of our dialogue and said we would figure it out.

By seven, I was in my new room alone. The room they put me in could have passed for a hotel room, and I appreciated the floor to ceiling view of the city at night. It overlooked the downtown area, and I could see the capital building in the distance. People below my window milled about, completely unaware that my future lay in the hands of the hospital.

I heard car horns honking and engines revving in the distance. The nurses showed me the kitchenette behind the nurses station and encouraged me to grab a drink or a snack when needed.

The neurologist on staff came in to introduce herself. She quickly reviewed the findings of the MRI and told me that the next day I would be meeting with a team of doctors and specialists. I gave vials of blood repeatedly throughout the night. Every few hours, I awoke to my nurse taking blood, checking my blood pressure, or forcing me to pee in a cup.

At five-thirty the following morning, I heard a knock on the door, and the bright overhead light flickered on. A group of people in lab coats surrounded my bed. They asked me to recite my story again, and shined a flashlight in my eyes. One of them pulled out an eye chart on their phone and I read the letters to the best of my ability. Within minutes they were gone.

Next came a young doctor from the Endocrinology department. I had never heard of endocrinology before, and I wasn't sure what kind of information they wanted. I recited my story again, and she asked me a variety of questions related to things I had never noticed: When was the last time you had your period? Tell me about the health of your nails and hair. Have you gained any weight over the past few years? Do you have a recent photo and a photo from a few years ago that I can see? Can I check you for stretch marks? How is your energy level?

I didn't understand what her questions had to do with a tumor on my optic nerve, but I answered her as best I could.

A few hours later, she returned. "Hi Ashley." She settled in the seat beside me and leaned forward. "We got your labs back, and your cortisol is much higher than we would have expected," she began. "We need to do some additional tests to rule out Cushing's disease. I need you to go off of your birth control because oral contraceptives can skew your cortisol level. Stop taking Biotin for your hair because that can skew lab results also." I didn't know what Cushing's was, but I made a mental note to google it later. "We will monitor your hormones while you're here and send you home with some additional labs to complete."

I nodded blankly. I couldn't remember her name.

"You have a huge tumor," she said. "It is very unusual because tumors that big do not typically cause increased hormone level, but your cortisol level has been consistently high."

Chapter 7

Grateful she provided information about my tumor, I leaned in to see her better. She told me that another doctor from her department would be checking in with me before I left the hospital.

The next doctor to come in was from the Neuro-Ophthalmology department. She looked at my eyes with a light, had me read her portable eye chart, and asked me questions related to my vision. The change was so gradual I hadn't noticed the impact.

That day, I traveled throughout the hospital for a CT scan and then another MRI to get a closer look at the tumor. After returning, I was wheeled to the Neuro-Ophthalmology department to meet with the Neuro-Ophthalmologist, Dr. Chalksky.

The receptionist brought me into a small room and took pictures of my eyes. Then I placed my face in a machine with each eye patched separately, and clicked a button every time I saw a light. The bright lights flashed and caused my eyes to water. He sent me to another floor to have an ultrasound done on my eyeballs.

After I returned to the main office, a tall man with a German accent and a younger man with glasses escorted me into the room. Again, I recited my story. I told them that it felt like only one eye was working at times, that when I looked at a word, the left half disappeared, and that sometimes my brain read a word wrong but kept the ending the same, like reading the word possibility as accountability. I told them that I felt dizzy at times or perceived the environment to be tilted. And geometric patterns danced.

I explained how I couldn't see anything after dusk and needed bright lights to help me navigate my house and that sometimes it felt like I was wearing sunglasses even though I wasn't. I told them everything was blurry at times, but it was inconsistent and depended on the day. And how I couldn't recognize my co-workers or the people at the technology competition. I told them about my headaches and how sometimes they were debilitating and other times a dull ache radiated between my ears or right above my eyebrows.

We completed another assessment in his office, similar to what I experienced with Dr. Ling. I read the numbers in the colorblind booklet and read the letters on the eye chart, and just like before, I struggled to identify the numbers and letters because the left half disappeared. I explained how when I read, I needed to move my eye gaze from the middle of the letter or number to the space directly to the left.

Dr. Chalksy held what looked like a giant ruler up to one eye and quickly transferred it back and forth to the other eye. I focused and identified the letter behind him, but it took a considerable amount of time for the image to come into focus. Lastly, he took a safety pin and poked me up and down both sides of my face and from my forehead to my ears to my nose. Certain pinpricks I could barely feel and other pinpricks were excruciating and caused me to jump in my chair.

While Dr. Chalksky assessed me, he communicated with the other doctor and explained why he was doing what he was doing. Finally, he said, "You have a large tumor sitting on your optic chiasm but more on the right. That is why you have a left periphery loss in both eyes. You also have pallor, which means your nerve is dying. You have permanent damage to your nerve." He showed me a circle graph with green, yellow, and red segments. The red components on both eyes indicated the loss of cellular life. "Your tumor is very big. We need to remove it, or you will go blind, and you will die." He turned to the younger doctor and said, "Without removal, it will grow out of her orbit."

I wasn't a doctor, but I knew he was referring to my eye socket, and sheer panic set in again.

"Are you still driving?" he asked.

I hesitated because I didn't want to hear the recommendation. "Yes," I said.

"Do you think you should be driving?" I was so overwhelmed with all the information thrown at me. Twenty-four hours ago, I was home and healthy. Kind of.

"I don't know," I answered. I wasn't going to volunteer not to drive.

"I don't think you should," he said bluntly. "It is not safe. We need to get the tumor removed first and then decide."

Exhausted and sad, the hospital employee transported back to my room in time for dinner. I called my husband and relayed all the information about

Chapter 7

the people I saw and tests I underwent that day.

"I'm coming tomorrow. My mom and dad are taking the kids to the Children's Museum and then out to dinner."

"What did you tell the kids?" I asked him.

"I told them you were in the hospital for a few days so the doctors could figure out why you were having so many headaches," he responded.

"Thank you. Did they take it okay?" I asked. I felt terrible not being home with them to comfort them if they were afraid.

"Robbie took it fine, but Alexandria was a little freaked out. She kept asking me when you were coming home and if you would be able to go to her Girl Scout meeting this week."

"Oh shoot. I completely forgot. We were going to complete our cooking badge outside on the campfire." Alex had been excited because she found a banana s'more recipe that she would demonstrate for the rest of the girls.

"I told her Jessica would take over if needed," Michael said. He was always one step ahead, solving problems before they evolved into a catastrophe.

"Thank you," I said again.

He sounded better today. He sounded less like a deer trapped in headlights and more like a superhero stepping into action. Without him here, I proved that I could be strong, and he could be strong without me. It allowed me to process the little information I had at my own pace without worrying about how he was processing the information as well. I knew having him home with the kids allowed me to focus on what I needed instead of their needs.

With that being said, I still missed him.

That night, I didn't sleep. The nurses woke me every few hours for labs and vitals. I fell in and out of sleep, wondering when I could go home and what the long-term plan would be. I restrained myself from googling anything about my condition until I had all the information.

Trusting they would tell me all I needed to know, I prayed to God requesting strength to spread over my family. I knew I needed to be strong and do whatever the doctors recommended, but I didn't know if I was mentally prepared for the long haul.

Chapter 8

I woke at six for labs, and at six-thirty the neurology team surrounded my bed, shining the light into my eyes and asking me to read the eye chart. Every time they visited, they stuck their fingers out to the sides of my head and asked if I could see their fingers moving. Every time I could, but every time the person placed his wagging fingers at different distances and angles from my face. Even I knew it wasn't an accurate assessment. The same was true for the eye chart. Sometimes it was an arm's length away, and sometimes it was a leg's length.

My husband arrived at ten on the dot. He carried a small vase behind his back filled with flowers, and when he approached the side of my bed, he yelled, "Surprise!" The beautiful bouquet lit up my room. He placed them on the counter across from my bed, kissed me, and sat on the couch next to me. "The kids wanted to get you something."

"That was so nice of them." Sadness crept into my heart because I hadn't been with them. Over the years, I had traveled for many business trips, but this trip was unplanned and chaotic. This trip to the hospital felt messy and indecisive.

I hoped the kids didn't sense the dread, fear, and confusion without me.

"I also brought you some clothes," Michael said. He placed a small tote on my lap. I dug through the bag, pulling out clean underwear, sweatpants, and a tank top.

Chapter 8

"Thank you. I've been dying to shower and get out of this hospital gown." I buzzed the nurse, and she helped wrap my IV so it wouldn't get wet in the shower. She showed me how to use the shower and requested I call her from the bathroom if there was an emergency.

I hadn't been on my feet in about twenty-four hours, and the room started to tip and tilt. She grabbed my arm and asked if I was okay, and I nodded. She looked at me as she considered if I was lying or well enough to shower on my own. Hesitating, she left me in the bathroom and told Michael to call if we needed anything.

When I got back to my bed, my fatigue diminished for the sheer fact that I was wearing my own comfy clothes. I hated wearing the hospital gown because it reminded me that something was wrong.

Long clumps of hair decorated the white pillowcase. I knew I lost a lot of hair in the shower, but in the shower, I tugged on my hair and ran my fingers from root to end when using conditioner. Losing hair in the shower felt acceptable, but losing hundreds of strands while barely moving felt obscene.

I pointed to the bed and said, "They asked me about my hair and nails yesterday. I guess this is what they were getting at."

Michael and I sat in silence with reality television playing in the background. I ordered enough food for lunch to satisfy both of us, but Michael refused to eat it.

"I'm not a patient," he said.

"So what? I ordered it for me, but it's too much. You should eat it."

We shared everything on the tray so he wouldn't feel guilty.

Various doctors and nurses continued to rotate in and out, checking my eyes, my vitals, drawing blood, and filling me in on the day. From the sounds of it, I still needed to meet with Occupational Therapy and the Neurosurgeon team.

After lunch, two women came in from Occupational Therapy. They listened to my story and explained the functional vision assessment. We walked to the kitchenette to make a peanut butter and jelly sandwich for their evaluation.

I stood in the kitchenette, opening drawers and cabinets, looking for the bread, peanut butter, jelly, and knife. I expected the peanut butter to be in a jar, the bread in a loaf, and the jelly in the refrigerator. I looked in all the appropriate places but couldn't find anything I needed.

The Occupational Therapy gave me hints. "The bread is in the refrigerator." I looked again but still didn't see it. She told me to scan left to right and top to bottom. Finally, on the top left, I saw a series of thin wax bags piled on top of each other. Inside each bag was one slice of bread. I took two bread bags out of the fridge and placed the bread on top of a plate.

"Now, peanut butter," I said to myself.

"Top shelf on the left," my navigator said. I opened the cabinet to the left of the sink and pulled down plastic containers with items inside. I didn't see anything that resembled peanut butter.

The Occupational Therapist told me to stand in front of the fridge and point to the cabinet on the left. I moved to my left about four steps and looked at the cabinets. There were three sets, but before, I had only seen two. I had omitted the farthest cabinet on the left when I stood in front of the sink. I opened up the most distant cabinet and pulled down a bucket. Inside were individually packaged jelly and syrup containers that you would find at the local diner.

"I don't see any peanut butter," I said to her, putting the bucket on the counter.

She pulled out the syrup and said, "What's this?"

"Syrup," I replied.

She told me to look again, and I picked up the syrup and read the top—peanut butter. The wrapping looked dark brown through my dying eyes.

I took the peanut butter and jelly and rummaged around until I found an individually wrapped knife. Finally, I finished my sandwich, shocked at my difficulty.

As we walked up and down the hallway, I told her every room number we passed. She encouraged me to physically turn my head at ninety degrees because my peripheral vision had diminished. I read the numbers, but it required all my attention due to the periphery loss and blurriness.

Back in the room, she asked how I thought the evaluation went. I

Chapter 8

admitted that I didn't realize how bad my eyes had gotten. We talked about accommodations at home to reduce the risk of falls and frustration. She told me that I frequently needed "missing" objects, such as the television remote, to be wrapped in white tape so I could see it in dim lighting. She recommended I keep things in the same place every day to know exactly where to find them. I needed to tape elevation changes, so I wouldn't trip. She advised me against driving.

I knew at the ophthalmologist's office that my vision was terrible. I hadn't realized how it affected my functioning until I failed to independently make a peanut butter and jelly sandwich.

Michael paid attention to her recommendations and agreed to follow all her suggestions. I sat on the couch next to him and looked around the room. I was so tired of analyzing my vision, but I couldn't stop. Hyperaware of my vision difficulties, I knew I had a long road ahead of me.

That afternoon, a tall woman with high heels, pearls, and a pencil skirt knocked on my door and walked into my room. "Hi, Ashley?" she asked.

"Hi," I nodded.

"My name is Dr. Walker, and I am a neurosurgeon."

I introduced her to my husband, and she sat down at the computer in the room. "Have neuro-ophthalmology, neurology, and neuro-endocrinology seen you?" she asked.

"Yes, and Occupational Therapy," I added.

"Oh great, what did they say?" she inquired.

"They said I shouldn't be driving, the tumor could make me go blind and kill me, and they are looking to see if I have Cushing's." Yes, those were the most significant blows I had heard over the course of my stay.

Dr. Walker smiled and typed into the keyboard. "Okay. Please come here so we can chat." She pulled up images of my brain, and pointed at the various shades of gray running throughout. "See that spot?" she pointed at a white blob with her cursor.

Michael and I nodded, not quite sure what the blob meant. "That is your tumor. It is rather large. You have probably had it for years and never even knew until it started to mess up your eyes." She changed the images to show me the tumor from different angles of my head. "We need to get it out."

"How?" I asked.

"Well, we can try to go up through your nose, but there is a chance we won't be able to get it all, and we will have to go through the top of your head. We really won't know until we are in there. Your tumor is big, but it looks fairly easy. I imagine the surgery through the nose will last a few hours."

I looked at Michael, and his face appeared taut with small creases popping up on his forehead. "When?" I asked.

"Well, that is up to you. We don't know for sure, but we think it is a pituitary adenoma, which means it is most likely benign."

I breathed a sigh of relief because she answered the question I was too afraid to ask.

"We can do it before Thanksgiving or after."

Without stopping to think, I blurted, "After." There was no way I was denying my family Thanksgiving.

"Okay, I will call you within the week with the day and time of your surgery. For these types of surgeries, I partner with the ENT, and we complete the surgery together. When I call, I will go over more in-depth what will happen and answer your questions."

I knew by the time she called, google searches in my computer and phone would be overwhelmed with the keywords "pituitary tumor," "transsphenoidal surgery," and "Cushing's Disease."

Just as quickly as she arrived, she was gone. I looked at Michael. I felt like we had no more information than we had before she arrived, yet somehow we had a plan. The tumor was hefty and needed to come out, but we didn't know what type of surgery would happen or when. I grabbed his hand and interwove my fingers into his. "I can't wait to go home," I whispered.

Chapter 9

I took a deep breath and quickly opened the door with a broad, bright smile on my face. "Happy Thanksgiving!"

Amanda and Steve stood on our doorstep with their two toddlers Jayce and Harper. Amanda held a large, brown, department store bag filled with store-bought food in one arm and a portable high chair in the other. Steve carried a rolled-up pack-n-play in one hand and a bag overflowing with toddler toys.

I thought back to when I had two toddlers and smiled in sympathy. I gave them a big hug, embracing all their belongings, and ushered them into the house. "Michael is in the kitchen if you want to drop off the food," I directed.

The brisk Thanksgiving air carried the scent of snow. Despite the constant darkness, difficulty seeing, and overall dread when the sun went down, this was my favorite time of year and my favorite holiday. I loved sharing a meal with family for the sole purpose of spending time together.

Growing up, our family ate Sunday Supper at my grandparents with my cousins, aunts, and uncles. Thanksgiving was the only day I could recreate that feeling. Of course, it wasn't really the same because we only saw our family under one roof twice a year. It had always been a little difficult to recreate coziness and comfort when we weren't as close, but those Sunday Suppers were one of my favorite childhood memories.

I closed the door, leaned against it, and stared through the foyer and into the kitchen. I heard Michael and Amanda struggle to put the food into the refrigerator, and I listened to the kids run from the kitchen to the great room. I told Alex and Robbie they were on kid duty until after dinner, and they happily obliged. Giving them fifteen dollars for their efforts probably helped persuade them, but I knew without a monetary bribe it would be a struggle to get them off video games.

The overwhelm and internal chaos I felt today seemed stronger than usual. In my pre-tumor life, I organized Thanksgiving in my sleep. I knew who was bringing the food, when to start the turkey, and how to create a warm, friendly, and inviting ambiance.

Right now, my head throbbed, the left side of my vision was fading, and I continuously bumped into furniture and walls. Ever since the ER visit, I stopped sleeping. I harbored a chest-crushing secret, and I didn't know how to rip the band-aid off and tell people that I was terrified I would die or would never be the same if I survived.

Michael and I had returned from the hospital six days before, and we debated what to do with Thanksgiving dinner and the family gathering. I couldn't process all the information thrown at me like darts. I didn't want to tell anyone until I understood what was happening.

We decided that maybe a final supper with the family would help take my impending doom away for a short while. We'd tell the kids once we had our plans solidified regarding the surgery and the recovery. I felt like I was living a nightmare, and if I just waited long enough, I would wake up with a start and go to work like any other day.

Jason, Melinda, and Ellie arrived next. Sometimes Jason visited Melinda's family, but for the most part, Ellie saw Amanda's kids just as frequently as mine did.

Ellie zoomed past to find Alexandria, and I gave Jason a big hug. His large body protected me from the cold, and I held on for a few seconds too long.

"I know it's been a long time," he said into my hair.

I felt one tear spill onto my cheek. "Let me take your coats," I said, pulling away from him, trying to control my emotions. I hugged Melinda and held onto her for just as long. I missed my brother.

Chapter 9

When we were kids, we spent all our time together. I would sneak into his bedroom at night and sleep in a sleeping bag on his floor because I was scared of the dark. Our parents got separated for a year when I was eleven. They eventually got back together, but it never felt the same.

During that year, Jason was my only ally. He understood my anxiety, fear, confusion, and despair when I couldn't verbalize my thoughts or feelings. He was fourteen at the time, and he had been my rock my entire life. When Michael and I got married, Michael became my rock, and Jason returned to being my brother.

I wanted to tell him my secret. I tried to open my mouth and have all my secrets spill out, but I couldn't. Thanksgiving was my favorite holiday of the year, and I couldn't dampen the mood with my medical problems. I wanted my kids to know before anyone else. For now, it was my little secret. I needed to pretend everything was fine, but I was struggling.

I heard car doors slam, and Janet, Hank, and Tiffany stood in the driveway, arguing. I heard words like "idiot!" and "honked!" and "light!" and knew that it had something to do with another driver.

Hank was from a different generation and believed that the man should always take care of the woman. In this case, that meant he should drive. We all knew he was almost seventy-five years old and shouldn't be driving, but every time the subject came up, Hank would storm away from the conversation.

Tiffany was in the car to act as a backseat driver to ensure their safety, but Hank and Janet didn't know that.

Tiffany saw me and waved. She raced toward me, ignoring her dad who was still complaining about the stop light incident. "Hi." She hugged me, and handed me a warm dish. "I brought dinner." She burst into the house, calling for Michael and Steve to help with Hank's stuff.

After everyone was inside, I closed the door and sneaked off into the bathroom in our master suite. I thought I could hide in there for a few minutes and refresh. I took some Advil, splashed water on my face, and sniffed my essential oils meant to calm and relax.

"Mooom! Mom?" It was Alexandria.

"Right here, honey!" I called out, hoping my voice sounded normal.

"Tabby threw up on the internet box." Tabby was our cat.

"Wait, what?" I asked.

"Tabby had a hairball and was sitting on the shelf with the modem, and she threw up all over it. Now the internet is out, and the kids are crying because they can't watch their shows. Uncle Steve is freaking out because he might not be able to watch football, and dad lost the recipes for dinner."

I grabbed my phone. Not only was Wi-Fi out, but our cellular data was spotty due to our spot in the woods. I knew the only way to get reception was to walk to the end of our driveway near the main road. We couldn't even go to the store to buy a new one because all the stores were closed.

"I'll be right down," I said

The TV said, "Poor Connection" across the screen. I disconnected the modem and cleaned the top. The internet must have died between the bile and water seeping inside the grooves.

Michael stood in the kitchen unpacking side dishes and desserts. Tiffany pulled out all our old cookbooks stored in the cabinet above the refrigerator that no one could reach. Janet and Hank sat at the kitchen table, watching the chaos.

The kids ran into the basement to play so they wouldn't be in the way, Jason and Steve rehashed the Patriots game from the week before, and Melinda and Amanda set up all the baby gear to get ready for nap time.

I cleaned the vomit, noticing the brown bile decorating my cream carpet. I made a mental note to have the cleaners come earlier than scheduled. For now, I moved the television armoire just a tad to cover it.

"Sorry, boys! No football today. You'll have to walk to the edge of the driveway with your phone if you get desperate." I said. "We have DVDs in the basement if the kids need to watch a movie," I told Amanda.

Amanda let everything roll off her shoulders and she nodded at me. She had two small kids, her shirts were always stained, wrinkled, and untucked, and the kids' hair was messy from sleep. She stopped working to stay home with them, yet she always had a smile on her face. I admired her perseverance, but I wondered if she was the type of mother who locked herself in the bathroom and guzzled vodka or cried in the shower.

Chapter 9

I watched Michael fumble with the seasonings in the kitchen, trying to remember the recipe.

"Michael, my grandmother used to take the bird and pour a can of coke over the top, an hour before it was done. It caramelizes the skin and sweetens the meat. Just do that. It's easy enough, and we need to get it in the oven if we're going to eat on time." I looked at the clock. Based on the events of the day, dinner would be delayed.

"Sounds good." He dumped seasonings on the bird and threw it in the oven.

"Do you need any help?" Tiffany asked. "You seem a little stressed out."

I ignored her comment and put a big smile on my face. "No, no. Everything is fine. I love hosting Thanksgiving, but you never know how the day is going to flow." I wondered if she could sense that something more than just Tabby's sickness was bothering me. I carried plates into the formal dining room where the vegetable and cracker plates sat half empty.

Tiffany followed me. "Hey," she called from behind me. "Are you sure you are okay? You seem like something is hanging over you lately."

"Oh no, I'm good. Work is good, kids are good, Michael is good. Everything is good." I said, my voice an octave higher. My hands shook as I placed the plates on the table.

"You say you are, but I've known you for decades now. You don't seem happy, and I just want you to know that I am here for whatever is going on."

I swallowed back my tears and went into the bathroom.

What did she mean, saying that I'm not happy? Of course, I'm happy. We have this beautiful home, I love my job, and my kids receive an excellent education. What would I not be happy about?

This was not the first time Tiffany approached me about confiding in her regarding my woes, but this was the first time it bothered me. *Was I happy?* I put on a fresh coat of lipstick and took a deep breath. I needed to get through the weekend.

Dinner went off without a hitch. The turkey was the best part of the entire meal. The juicy and tender meat harmonized with the crispy, sweet skin. I didn't know why we didn't use this turkey trick in years past.

The tryptophan kicked in, the adults got sleepy, and when the sugar from the desserts kicked in, the kids got wild. The clean-up was always worse than the cooking.

I had run the dishwasher before dinner because the cups, serving plates, and appetizer plates were aplenty. After the meal, I had a mountain of dirty dishes piled beside me on the stove and all available counters. I had always wanted a larger kitchen with a massive island, but our kitchen just wasn't built that way.

The quiet dishwasher indicated it was done cleaning. I unpacked the silverware. I found an occasional spoon that didn't get clean or a knife with grease shining in the light. One by one, I pulled out the dirty silverware, and I questioned the probability. I had never had to throw back so many dirty items. I pulled open the top rack, and none of the glasses held the small reservoir of water along the cups base.

Wait a minute! I know I turned this on. I checked the detergent reservoir, eyeing the closed cap. *Ugh! I never turned it on. How did that happen? I never forget to turn on the dishwasher! I run dishes every single day. I have a system and a routine that never fails.*

I stood alone in the kitchen and quickly reloaded the silverware that had made its way back into the drawer and pressed start. Once I heard the machine kick on, I looked around at the disaster that would take over my kitchen for the next four hours.

To help create order, I scraped the food off all plates either into the trash can or garbage disposal, stacked the same sized plates together, and washed all the pots and pans by hand. Even though the clean pots and pans took up the same amount of space as the dirty ones, I felt much more in control with clean and drying dishes.

I remained attentive to my guests the rest of the night but still couldn't quite figure out how I hadn't started the dishwasher. These forgetful moments happened more and more, and I couldn't help but wonder if the tumor was pressing on the part of my brain that helped me organize my day and get things done. If it was permanent damage, I was in big trouble because I couldn't do my job without multitasking. I had dedicated so many hours of

Chapter 9

my life to work and had created respect among my coworkers; I didn't know who I was without my job.

Work had become intertwined with my identity. I had no idea what the future would bring, but I was afraid that the comfort of the life we had created was on the brink of collapse. I distracted myself from my thoughts with a glass of red wine.

On my third glass, the buzz of conversation quieted my thoughts.

Chapter 10

Three days of hosting were two days too long. The day after Thanksgiving, I went Black Friday shopping with the girls and somehow lost my wallet. I panicked at the register as I emptied my purse on the counter.

It turned out, my black wallet rested on the black counter to my left and I didn't see it. Melinda gently picked it up and gave it to me without saying a word, but I saw the questioning look in her eyes.

I usually loved Black Friday shopping. The thrill of getting a good deal superseded the dread of waking up at four in the morning. On previous Black Friday mornings, I listed all the stores I wanted to hit up in sequence, depending on the sales and the big-ticket items up for grabs.

This year, Melinda and Tiffany stood in the kitchen waiting for me to tell them our itinerary. Amanda and Janet usually came too, but Amanda needed to stay home this year because of the kids, and Janet had a bad hip. They were dumbfounded when I told them that I hadn't prepared a list or even looked at the flyers. The success of this day was dependent upon the plan.

Today, there was no plan.

We started at Kohl's because Kohl's was closest to the house, and we all had Kohl's Cash burning in our pockets. The line to get into the store wrapped down the sidewalk past four additional storefronts. "I guess we should have gotten here earlier," I said to Tiffany and Melinda.

Chapter 10

"I have the flyer right here. Let's look through and figure out our plan of attack." Melinda took over my role as head-honcho. We skimmed the sales pages, but the dim lighting and small print made my head hurt directly in between my eyes. I couldn't look anymore, so I listened to their suggestions and blindly agreed.

We slowly snaked our way into the store and split up with a plan to meet back at the registers in thirty minutes. I found some toys for the kids, a new jacket for myself, and clothes for everyone in my family. I mentally added how much money I was spending on my overflowing cart, and hoped I hadn't gone over budget.

I found the girls at the front of the store, and it appeared that they also had a successful shopping endeavor. Tiffany's cart contained more items for herself than anyone else because she didn't have a significant other or children. Melinda filled her carriage with necessities, like socks, underwear, slippers, and coats. We chatted about our deals as the line to check out crept forward.

When it was my turn to pay, not only did I lose my wallet, but I completely messed up my payment. Every Black Friday, I dropped about a thousand dollars between all the stores, and I needed to remain organized. To do this, I paid with a check at every store because my checkbook had the carbon copy underneath. It made adding up my totals easier.

I took out my checkbook and filled out the date. After handing the cashier my Kohl's rewards card, I realized I never put my wallet back in my bag. My brain switched from writing out my check to searching for my wallet to rewriting my check. I handed it to her, and she looked at me.

"Ma'am," she said. I hated when people called me Ma'am. "Your check isn't filled out correctly."

I looked at the check, which read $3,356.84. *Ugh*! I must have written the three, gotten distracted by my wallet, and then re-written the number without seeing that I already wrote a three.

I saw Melinda and Amanda waiting for me near the door, wondering what was going on.

"I'm so sorry," I said to the cashier. "I'm having some vision problems.

Here. Let me give you my card." I took the check, ripped it in half, and made a mental note to write down my Kohl's amount in my budget. I smiled at the girl and walked out of the store as if nothing had happened.

When my family asked what had taken so long, I brushed it off and said I misplaced my card, which was true. We traveled around that morning, hitting up all the big stores with the sales. By eight o'clock, our rubbery legs ached, the car was stuffed with bags and gifts, and my shopping list was almost done.

I picked up a few items for myself because the prices were just that good, and I secured a new modem on sale, so we would have Wi-Fi at the house again.

When we made it back to the house, we transferred all our packages to the appropriate trunks and headed inside.

The place was noisy, messy, and chaotic. People, toys, and plates were everywhere. Breakfast plates, half mugs of coffee, and overflowing trash cans littered the kitchen. As the hostess, I swallowed my annoyance and cleaned.

After lunch, we drove to the Christmas tree farm in the next town. My children loved picking out their Christmas tree. Alexandria's favorite holiday was Christmas, and she always picked out a mini-tree for her bedroom, and Robbie helped pick out the ten-footer for our great room.

We went to this farm for years and set up a tree delivery service so our Range Rover wouldn't get scratched during the transport home. We all split up into our respective families in search of the perfect holiday tree. All trees would be delivered the next day before the family dispersed.

"Mom!" Alexandria called out. She was deep in the rows of trees, standing beside a four-foot pear shaped fir. Extra long branches stuck out along the bottom and short stubby branches along the top. It almost looked like someone took a hedge trimmer to the top half and forgot about the base.

"Really?" I asked. "Don't you want to find one a little more uniform?"

"No, this one is perfect because it isn't perfect," Alex persuaded.

"Okay," I shrugged. "Sounds good to me." I took the tag and brought it to the farmer for safe keeping.

Chapter 10

Alex and I found Michael and Robbie examining a tall, fat tree on the other side of the farm. It towered over my six-foot-tall husband and was wide enough to wrap him in a hug. The needles had a blue tint to them, and the branches stood strong and straight.

"Perfect," Michael said, gazing at the beautiful tree.

"This is the one we picked out," Robbie proudly stated. He grabbed the tag to bring it to the farmer. We sat in the farmhouse and enjoyed hot apple cider and apple cider donuts until the rest of the family arrived.

The room started spinning ever so slightly. I felt like my right eye was working, but my left eye remained dead, dragged through life by the stronger twin. As a result, the room tipped a bit, and I closed my eyes to reset the experience.

I used my downtime looking around the farmhouse. I looked at my family, and still, the right side of their face jumped out at me, and the left remained muted in the background. I looked at the signs across the room, and read "FFEE," "ARM OSE," and "STMAS EES." The entire left side of the words had disappeared. Looking forward and out the corner of my eyes, everything remained blurry unless I looked straight forward.

I covered my eyes with my hands like a telescope, and suddenly the words read "COFFEE," "FARM HOUSE," and "CHRISTMAS TREES."

It was so perplexing. I didn't understand what was happening to me. I felt my spirits sink as I pondered why my brain was failing me. The overwhelming dread of my future covered me like a thick fog. I sat in silence, lost in my thoughts, until the rest of the family arrived. When they did, I plastered a big smile on my face, hoping that my mood didn't ruin their weekend.

Back at home, the family cuddled on the large sectional couch and overstuffed chairs watching Christmas movies. This, too, had become another family tradition. I couldn't concentrate on the film, so I headed upstairs to relax in my room. I knew I had ninety minutes before the movie was over, and ninety minutes was just enough time to put my anxious mind to rest over my upcoming surgery.

In two weeks, I would fall asleep praying to wake up healthy. December tenth was surgery day and exactly five weeks from the hospitalization that no one knew about, except Michael and Jessica.

Navigating work had been tricky. I was afraid to tell them the whole truth because I wanted to believe that I was indispensable. If someone else took my job, I didn't know how I would take it. Instead, I told them that I needed to take a few weeks off for FMLA due to a family illness, which was partly true. I submitted the paperwork to human resources and knew that if anyone found out the details, HR would violate HIPPA.

I was scheduled to go back Monday and knew I had to tell them the whole truth.

My neurosurgeon said I would be out of work for three weeks to recover. She said it depended on the person, and some return as early as two weeks or as late as six or eight weeks. My tumor seemed easy enough, so she thought three would be appropriate. That would put us at the New Year. *God, I hoped 2020 was better than 2019.*

She explained to me that they would be going up my nose to get the tumor out. She explained that most tumors are soft, so it pops and can be suctioned out in small pieces when punctured. The ENT surgeon would be there, too, because they would need to get behind the sinus cavity to the pituitary gland. She explained that one potential risk was a cerebrospinal fluid leak, which could lead to meningitis. Nose drips that resembled a leaky faucet were reason to go back to the Emergency room.

Dr. Walker explained that I would go to a recovery room, possibly even ICU, and then move to a regular room for a day or two after surgery. Most people were out of the hospital within two days. She explained that I would mostly be followed by Neuro-Ophthalmology for my eyes and Neuro-Endocrinology for my hormones. She sounded confident that things would be easy.

I pulled out a notebook and pen and started writing down all the obstacles this surgery presented for our family. *First, childcare. Who was going to watch the kids while Michael and I were at the hospital? Second, childcare during my recovery. Would I need someone home with me too?*

I wrote down **WILL, Health Care Proxy, and Advanced Directives** to

Chapter 10

remind myself that I needed to pull out all those documents.

I wrote **Christmas**. Afraid I wouldn't be myself by Christmas, and the kids would have a dismal holiday, I needed a Plan B. Christmas would be exactly two weeks post-surgery, so hopefully, I would be better by then.

I needed to get my work stuff in order. I wrote **Money** and **School** because I had to inform the school what was going on, just in case the kids responded poorly to the news. Finally, the chaos swirling in my head started to subside, but the headache in between my eyebrows began to rise. *Maybe it was too much on my eyes to read and write with so little sleep and not enough water.*

I lay in my bed and tried to nap until the movie ended, and my family ran around the house like maniacs. I realized that Michael and I couldn't do this thing, this disruptive event, alone. I had my entire family here until tomorrow.

I decided to break the news after the kids went to bed in one fell swoop. I felt like the girls were onto me anyway. We had to see who could help because we wouldn't survive without emotional and physical support from others.

That night, the kids watched a movie on the projector in the basement, and the adults sat around the fireplace drinking decaffeinated Hot Toddy's. The whiskey warmed our souls, and the dancing flames warmed our bodies. I had told Michael that we needed to tell them tonight because I was scared that we wouldn't pull it off without their help.

"Cheers," I said, raising my glass. "To family." Everyone raised their glasses and clinked. The crackling of the logs filled the cathedral ceilings and caused a slight echo off the peak of the ceiling.

I didn't know if it was the exhaustion of the weekend or the inhibition of the alcohol, but I closed my eyes and opened my mouth. "I have a brain tumor," I said into the silence.

No one moved, no one said a word, and no one reacted. We continued to sit in a circle of silence, so I continued. "It's sitting on my optic nerve, so my vision is messed up. It explains all my headaches too. I'm having it removed in two weeks in Boston."

The finality of my plans was what broke the calm. I could hear the fear and confusion in people's voices, and I was afraid that the level of concern would result in me having a panic attack.

"You're the first people to know. We have no idea what we're going to do, but we have ten days to figure it out."

There were lots of questions thrown at us, and we didn't know how to answer them. I told them about all the weird symptoms I was having, how I ended up at the ER, and what the doctors said. I felt like I was regurgitating it again for a new medical professional.

I remained strong and reminded them that the kids didn't know. Michael and I would break the news after learning the details. We didn't want to increase their fear or worry.

After the movie ended and the big kids emerged from the basement, the nine of us had a skeleton of a plan. Tiffany would stay with us for one week after my surgery to help Michael with the kids. She couldn't afford to take more than one week off for vacation but told us that her job was flexible and she would come the day I went into the hospital to watch over Alex and Robbie.

Jason and Melinda lived too far to be a physical help but agreed to email grocery store gift cards. Michael and I appeared comfortable financially to the outside eye, but we had no savings, and without me working for a month or more, we weren't as secure as we pretended to be.

Janet and Hank offered to take the kids on the weekends, as long as the snow didn't make the drive up and down southern New England impossible.

Amanda and Steve were a young family, also struggling to make ends meet, and I knew they felt guilty for not providing a service like the others. Amanda volunteered to drive Alex and Robbie to Janet and Hank's house and pick them up for us on the weekends.

Michael and I accepted everything they were willing to offer.

I felt somewhat better but still overwhelmed. I had written everything down in a notepad because I knew I would forget between my brain and the whiskey.

That night, I climbed into bed and kissed Michael. "Thank you," I whispered. I still couldn't believe this was our life.

Chapter 11

"So, what did the kids say?" Jessica asked over our weekly breakfast. There were flakes in the air, and the sky was gray and dismal.

"I mean, what could they say? They said okay, and they listened to the plan." I shrugged my shoulders.

My kids were eight and eleven. I knew they were scared and probably didn't know what to do with their feelings. "We told them I had to have surgery because I had something the size of a grape growing in my head, and we had to get it out. I told them Auntie Tiff would be there until I came home and for a few days after that, and Michael would be in and out as well. I'll be tired when I come home from the hospital but I should be back to my normal self quickly." I knocked on the wooden window sill to make sure I didn't jinx myself.

"I'll be there too, you know. Anything you need, I'll be there." Jessica squeezed my hand in a motion of support. After a few beats of silence, she said, "And what about work? What did they say?"

I groaned. Work was the last group of people I wanted involved in this mess. I told them what was going on because I had no idea when I would be returning. "They couldn't say anything. I transferred all my projects to this new guy, William, and Karen went with him. Karen is my saving grace. She knows the projects just as well as I do, so I'm confident they won't screw up my accounts too badly. Work told me to take my time and heal, but I think they are obligated to say that shit."

"Did you figure out the money thing?" Jessica probed.

I shrugged my shoulders again. "Not really. I'm taking FMLA for four weeks, but hopefully, I'll be back to work before using up all my time. My plan is return to work for the new year. New year, new me. It's going to be tight between the mortgage and utilities, Christmas, and kids' activities, but we'll figure it out." I took a sip of my coffee, but the drafty window had already chilled the liquid.

"Let's see…." I saw Jessica's wheels turning, making sure she considered each obstacle. "Kids, check. Work, check. Money, check. Did you tell the school?"

I was relieved Jessica hadn't heard rumors about me in the hallway or lunchroom because I had met with the school the week before. I met with the principal, teachers, and social workers and rehashed my story three more times. Of course, when you say, "I have a brain tumor," everyone's demeanor changes because they feel sorry for you. They try to hide it because they don't want to make you feel more scared about something out of your control.

"I did. They've all been great. Mrs. Berry will check in on the kids once a week until I return to work. They asked about finances, which I felt uncomfortable answering, but at this point, why sugarcoat anything. I can't change it, so I shouldn't pretend that I can. They signed up the kids for free breakfast and lunch, free after school program, free before school program, and also put them on the Holiday gift drive."

"Mrs. Berry is awesome." Jessica said.

I had never met Mrs. Berry before because my kids never had a reason to see the school adjustment counselor, but she was warm, accepting, and understanding. She put so many of my hidden fears at ease. My biggest fear was that the kids wouldn't have a good Christmas because I couldn't spend unnecessary money beyond what I bought on Black Friday. When I showed Michael what I bought, his eyes bulged, and he pursed his lips. I knew from his body language alone that maybe I bought more than we could afford.

"I still can't believe my kids are getting free lunch—I kind of feel like a fraud. We live in a beautiful thirty-four hundred square foot house. Our

Chapter 11

car costs more than some people make a year. How can I be taking these supports from someone who needs them?" I asked, searching for validation in accepting the school's generosity.

"But you will need it, Ash," Jessica said. "You can't survive on Michael's salary alone, and what will happen if you can't go back to work? Don't turn your hand away until you truly can. Everyone understands, and no one needs to know the details. We all go through trying times. Trust me. I was there. I got food from food banks and had rent assistance because I had nothing to my name when I left George. Just me and Malia. I had to take care of her, no matter what that meant. The same is for you. There is no shame in accepting help. Your health and your family are your number one priority."

I felt lucky to have a best friend like Jessica. She always eased my fears, supported me, and loved my kids like they were her own. I knew that I had an immense hurdle to face in my personal life, but I also knew that it would be okay with Jessica and Michael by my side. I had a village behind me, ready to lift me when needed. I hoped that I was as good a friend to them as they were to me.

In four days, my life would spiral out of my control, and all I could do was hold on until the storm passed. All the noise swirling in my head about protecting my family from the after effects of this tumor, protecting our financial legacy, and getting back to work would be in full swing, and the chaos would turn into a twister.

Part Two

When life knocks you down, get back up. Your family is watching.
—E.D. Hackett

Chapter 12

Michael and I sat in the waiting room, my body ready to eject itself from the chair as soon as the receptionist called my name. I had been waiting to hear my name by far too many doctors within the past few months. I ran my hand over the packed hospital bag next to me, filled with toiletries, pajamas, and a tablet.

The waiting room had filled with people of all ages, and I wondered why they were there. The receptionist gave me a beeper, similar to what you would get at a restaurant when waiting for your table. We sat in anticipation, nervously waiting to feel the vibrations in our palm.

Tiffany was arriving tomorrow morning after work to help us take care of the kids. Last night, we dropped the kids with Jessica and Malia. I checked my watch.

"The kids should be in school. Do you think they're okay?" I asked.

"They're fine." Michael's gruff voice reminded me that he was scared, too.

The kids seemed okay when I said goodbye to them this morning. Robbie gave me a one-armed hug, and Alex gave me a bear hug. Alex had many questions about what was happening today, and I answered them as best I could. It was nearly impossible, though, because I didn't understand all the terms the doctors used or how to explain them to a child. To get through the fear, I told myself that I was in one of the best hospitals in the world. They had to know what they were doing.

Michael placed an overnight bag next to him as well. He was staying in the city for the next few days to be with me during my initial recovery. Guilt for making him go through my recovery alone sat in the tiny crevices of my mind. Sure, it would be terrifying for me, but I would be asleep the whole time. He would be sitting and waiting and watching the time tick by.

He held my hand in the waiting room and stroked my arm with his other hand. Fear consumed me over what the next three days would bring. I hadn't slept, I couldn't stop playing worst case scenarios in my head, and my body jumped at every sensation.

I researched my diagnosis online and read up on all the things that could go wrong during surgery. Blindness. Spinal fluid leak. Death. I prayed that Dr. Walker knew what she was doing.

I couldn't show Michael I was afraid because I needed him to be strong for the kids. His humor and confidence during difficult situations was something that had attracted me to him decades before. Our current situation was too scary to discuss, and I was fearful he would break under the consequences of a surgery gone wrong.

I hated that he was alone.

We sat in silence, waiting for my turn. We looked at the others in the room, the buzzer, the clock, our phones, or anything that would distract us from having to say goodbye. I felt naked without my hair done or contacts in, my pajamas on, and pocketbook at home. My phone, license, and insurance card were the only identifying information I had and tucked tightly into my toiletry bag.

My stomach growled. I had been up since five-thirty this morning and hadn't had a bite to eat since dinner the night before.

BZZZZ-BZZZZZ. Michael and I jumped out of our chairs to see where we were going next. The black and red square danced on the table, forcing me to move into autopilot.

The nurse whisked us down a long hallway, took my vitals, and gave me a blue and white hospital gown. She reviewed my surgery and all the potential side effects, including death.

My heart stopped beating and my lungs deflated, the consequences setting

Chapter 12

in.

"Do you have any questions?" she asked.

"No." Actually, I did, but I couldn't formulate the words.

Michael and I sat in another holding pattern. The nurses popped in and told me various reasons why we were late. We needed an available room in the Operating Room…we needed transportation to come…we needed the doctor to stop in before we could proceed.

We waited and waited. A small television played in the corner, and I tried to watch it but my brain couldn't focus. It was now two o'clock, and my surgery was supposed to have already started. My stomach flipped as I realized something could have gone wrong.

We continued to sit in the makeshift room with nowhere to go.

At two-thirty, someone arrived with a wheelchair to transport me to the Operating Room. I asked the nurse if Michael could come with me, and she said no.

He leaned over, kissed me, and squeezed my hand. "I'll see you when you wake up," he said.

My heart raced as I traveled down the long, sterile corridor alone. The man pushing me in the wheelchair tried to make small talk, but I wasn't in the right frame of mind.

The last stop before the actual operating room was another small holding cell. Dr. Walker entered, wearing blue scrubs and pearl earrings. She told me we were waiting for a space to open, and we were next. She reviewed the surgery with me, explaining that I had a 3X3 cm tumor pressing on my optic nerve. They believed it was a pituitary adenoma but weren't sure. The pathology report would determine the tumor type.

"Vision loss, hormone loss, pituitary dysfunction, and death might all occur," she reviewed.

I signed the waiver.

"Don't be alarmed if you wake up in the ICU," she said. "It might mean we had to go in and do a craniotomy, or it might mean there wasn't a bed open on the regular floor. Just be aware that it is possible." She repeated that we were doing the transsphenoidal surgery, which was through-the-nose.

There was still a chance they would have to go through my skull, but they wouldn't know until they were in there, poking around in my head.

My life was at the mercy of their hands, and if I wanted my sight back, this was the uncertain route I had to take.

Dr. Scully, the ENT, came in next and introduced himself. "Sorry we haven't met before. I didn't realize we hadn't met until two days ago when I saw your name on my schedule." He proceeded to tell me his role in the surgery. He would create a hole so the instruments could get into the space behind my sinus cavity and remove the tumor. He would then patch the hole, if needed, with skin from my abdomen. The amount of required penetration would determine if I needed a patch. If the patch failed, I would have a cerebrospinal fluid leak, so I needed to be concerned if I noticed a clear, constant drip.

I nodded and swallowed. Dr. Scully handed me a waiver saying that I was aware of the risks, and I signed.

The nurses popped in and out of my room and gave me the remote control for the television. Dr. Walker came in again and asked if she could call Michael, who was waiting for me, thinking I was already mid-surgery.

He must have been a wreck.

My cell phone was in my overnight bag, probably in a locker somewhere, so I rattled off his number.

"Hi Michael! It's Dr. Walker here…. yes, she's here. She's doing well. We've been a bit behind today, and we're still waiting to start. I'll call you or have one of the nurses call when we begin….yes. I assume a few hours after that….yes….okay, great. Talk to you then." She hung up the phone and told me it would be a few more minutes.

Now on a hospital gurney, I lay on my back as they wheeled me down a series of white hallways. The bright, fluorescent lights zipped by me, as the ceiling was the only thing I could see. The nurses quieted as we approached the operating room.

Just past the initial double doors, I entered a room with a series of computers, images of brains on the screen, and several people looking at the pictures. I saw a Dunkin Donuts styrofoam cup and a cell phone out of the

Chapter 12

corner of my eye sitting on the desk. I was starving, but the butterflies in my stomach hid my innate desire to eat. It had been seventeen hours since I last ate or drank, and I sensed my body was angry.

People raced around the operating room. The nurses and anesthesiologists introduced themselves to me like a movie montage in fast forward.

Someone placed a mask over my head and told me to count backward from one hundred.

I stared up at the bright light above my head and started counting. As I counted out loud, the people in the room popped in and out of my sight. I think I got to ninety-three, and then I was out.

*****

"Ashley….Ashley…." I heard my name called from a faraway place. I wanted to respond, but I couldn't open my eyes or move my lips.

"I'm here!" my inner voice called out. My mouth didn't move, and no one heard me. I tried to nod my head or wiggle my fingers to let them know I was awake and listening, but my brain could not communicate with my body. My head ached, and I wanted to open my eyes, but my brain wasn't strong enough to make that happen.

"Is she okay?" Michael asked.

"I'm here. I'm okay." My inner voice responded, but again, no one heard me. I still couldn't see him, but I knew he was there. The nurse flushed out my IV and injected me with something. The burning coursed through my veins and up and down my body. I held my breath until the burning subsided and hollered, *"Ow! Please stop! That hurts!"* but I was the only one who heard.

"She'll be fine. The doctor will be in in a moment to speak with you," the nurse responded. I assumed she was talking to Michael.

Someone placed their hand in mine, and I could feel the warmth penetrate my cool skin. "Ashley, if you want me to stay, squeeze my hand," I heard Michael say to me.

"Please don't go!" my inner voice screamed. I didn't think I could squeeze his hand, even if I tried. I did try, but nothing happened. I tried again. *"Please don't go!"*

"Oh, she'll be fine," I heard a female voice say. "She's in ICU, the nurses will care for her around the clock, and honestly, she won't remember any of this. There isn't room in here for you to stay. It's late. It's after midnight. Go and get a good night's rest. She'll be here tomorrow."

After a moment, Michael released my hand, and I heard movement around me. The nurse added, "The doctor is right outside and ready to speak with you."

"*No!*" my inner voice hollered. *"Please don't leave me here!"* I felt a kiss on my forehead and heard feet shuffling away from me, probably out the door. Then I heard nothing but the occasional beeping of the machines in my room.

That night was brutal. Every time the nurse drew blood or pushed medicine through my veins, my body burned with an out of control fire. The burning in my throat lingered with every swallow and I recognized the metallic taste of blood. Tears climbed behind my eyes.

I knew I was in ICU, but I didn't know why. *Was it because something went wrong?* The surgery was supposed to be over within a few hours, but it was the next day. *Did I have a craniotomy?*

I tried to touch my head, but my arms stayed frozen at my side. Something didn't feel right, but my mind was a jumbled mess. I tried to sleep, but I felt like a living zombie between my scorched throat, and burning veins. The constant vital checks, vision checks, and coming down from anesthesia kept my head awake while my body slept.

Every time a nurse came in to give me medication, I had to sit up, and every time I sat up, the room started to tilt and spin viciously. My belly flip-flopped against my chest, and I closed my eyes to subside waves of nausea. The nurse reassured me, saying that the sickness was par for the course from the anesthesia.

I called out to her, my voice scratchy and hoarse, quickly asking for a bucket. "I'm sick," I said.

She placed a pink bedpan under my mouth, and I emptied my blood-filled stomach. I opened my eyes in the dark room and saw the brick red liquid slosh around the shallow container. My throat burned like an inferno, and I cried hot tears. I couldn't lift my head, so I cried into my lap, as the nurse hurried into the bathroom to dump the blood.

The following day, I regained control of my eyes, but I couldn't wear my glasses. My head ached with increased intensity when I placed the lenses over my eyes. My heart sank when I realized I didn't feel any different. My vision wasn't any better, my throat still burned, the taste of blood lingered, and I couldn't project my voice beyond a whisper.

Doctor after doctor came in to check on me and give me an update. Dr. Scully reported with a smile that he didn't have to pack my sinuses or use my abdomen to seal the incision.

"You're still at risk for having a cerebrospinal leak, but the risk is negligible," he said.

The blood I continued to swallow came from the incision he made to get to the pituitary mass. He said no lifting, no straws, and no blowing my nose for the next three weeks. His kind eyes and soothing voice immediately put me at ease when he told me I should recover quickly.

The Endocrinology team came in next and reviewed all my lab work. In November, they told me to go off my birth control because it elevated my cortisol level. This time, they told me my cortisol hormone, which controls many things, such as energy level, fatigue, weight loss/gain, and the fight or flight stress response, was deficient. They prescribed me daily steroids to mimic cortisol in my body. My estrogen was also inadequate, but they didn't want to treat it until I allowed my ovaries to wake up from being suppressed by birth control for almost twenty-five years.

"Everything else looks great," the doctor said.

Dr. Walker came in last and told me that the surgery had lasted seven hours, and the tumor consistency was not what she expected.

"It was fibrous and difficult to remove," she said.

I allowed the words to float around me, my brain connecting the dots.

"We didn't have the proper tools available to remove such a fibrous mass. We got enough of a sample to biopsy but were unable to remove it."

My heart sank and boiled with anger. I wanted to lash out at her for not doing her job, but my throat was so raw, all I could do was cry silent, hot tears. I turned my head away from her so she wouldn't see my vulnerability.

"The good news," she said, "was that the initial pathology showed a benign pituitary adenoma, which means no cancer."

I nodded slowly, still processing that I had just gone through hell for nothing.

"We need to go back in."

I continued to face the wall with my eyes closed. I sensed the room tip and turn and my stomach somersaulted inside my abdomen. I couldn't do this again. There was so much I wanted to say, but all I could do was frown and try to swallow the lump in my throat, despite the pain.

"I need to go back in," she repeated. "I now know what the tumor looks like and feels like. I will ask my colleague to assist because he has a history of successful removal of tough tumors. I am confident that if we go in again, we can get it."

I could see the sympathy in her crinkled forehead, pursed lips, and searching eyes. I didn't believe her. I just wanted to go home. All of this agony, for nothing. I refused to make eye contact or acknowledge her, and she retreated into the hallway.

Feeling sick, I wasn't sure if it was because of the anesthesia, the surgery, or the news that I would have to relive the past twenty-four hours again.

I tried to think about my kids, but my thoughts jumbled into a pile of jigsaw puzzle pieces. I didn't know when I could go home, if more tests were needed, or how many more doctors I would see. I still couldn't talk or walk to the bathroom alone.

I slept on and off most of the day, and when I woke up for yet another blood draw, I saw Michael sitting in the folding chair next to me with concern all over his face.

I smiled and whispered hello with a slight wave. The dizziness started again, so I closed my eyes to stop it before it got out of control.

"Hi." He rubbed my arm. "How are you?"

"Awful," I mumbled. "I'm nauseous and dizzy, and last night I vomited all the blood sitting in my stomach. All I did last night was swallow blood." I shivered at the memory.

Chapter 12

"I'm so sorry. Are you feeling any better?" he asked gently.

I shook my head no. "Thankfully, I'm not still swallowing blood, but I can't eat or drink. My throat burns every time I swallow. I'm still nauseous, but the nurse said it's normal. Did you talk to the doctor?" I whispered to him.

He nodded, not quite sure how to proceed. "Did you?" he asked.

I nodded back at him. "Yeah. The surgery wasn't successful."

"That's not what she said to me. She said that they got enough to biopsy, and it isn't cancer," he said.

I knew I should have been happy that the C-word wasn't changing our lives forever, but I still felt half-dead both physically and mentally. "But they have to go in again." I interrupted him, feeling the tears spill down my cheeks again.

"Yeah, but Ash, she knows what she's getting herself into. She was in your head for seven hours. She knows what it looks like and where it is and how to approach it. She told me they didn't have the proper tools ready, which interfered with how much progress she could make. Think of this one as a dress rehearsal. Now they know what to do for the actual show."

My life is not theater. I glared at him in dissatisfaction. "She said she's going to ask someone for help," I said.

"Yeah, and do you know who she asked? The head of the department. She probably trained under him. I know it sucks, but we will get this thing out of your head no matter what. You're at one of the best hospitals in the world. If she couldn't get it out on the first try, imagine what would have happened if you had this done at a hospital closer to home." Michael was always so cheerful when I was down, but he had a point.

"I'm still in ICU," I said, keeping my eyes closed. The sky outside was darkening, and I didn't know if the sun was rising or setting.

"Yeah, but only because they didn't have a bed available at midnight last night."

"What time is it anyway?" I asked the airspace in front of me.

"Five p.m. They're probably bringing up dinner soon," Michael responded.

I nodded. "When am I going home?"

"I don't know. Probably tomorrow if everything checks out and you're feeling better."

I was nervous about going home because I didn't want to get sick again. I was afraid that I would trigger a cerebrospinal fluid leak by tipping my head down. *What if it happened tomorrow or the next night and I didn't recognize the signs? How would I know to go to the hospital?*

"How are the kids?" I asked, changing the subject. I knew they were with Tiffany, the fun, young, single aunt, but I was scared that they were frightened without us.

"They're okay. Tiff said they ordered pizza last night, and she took them to the movies today to kill some time. She's handling it. She's feeding them and keeping them alive, which is what we need, right?"

I cracked a smile. *If I were home, the kids would have read for twenty minutes, practiced their instruments, and done their chores.* I sighed, resigning to the fact that I was not in charge this week, and I didn't have a say in what they were doing right now. Michael was right. They were fed and alive.

"Tell them I'll call them tomorrow if I feel better. Tell them I love them, and I miss them," I requested.

"Will do," Michael nodded.

Dinner came, but I couldn't eat anything. The ICU room wasn't nearly as nice as the room from my first visit. Michael sat in a folding chair next to me, often standing to get out of the nurse's way.

My fatigue and nausea waned, and the medications they put me on made me tired. Michael and I sat together for a while, but I fell asleep.

When the nurse woke me up for my next round of blood draws and vital checks, he was gone.

Chapter 13

"No bending or lifting. No straws. Rinse out your sinuses daily. Take Tylenol for the headaches, as needed. Call me if you feel any dripping from your nose that is constant, clear, and watery. Call if you have any questions or concerns or if your vision gets worse."

The nurse organized my medication and reviewed my discharge papers. I didn't have any questions because I didn't know what to expect for today or tomorrow. I figured that whatever I was feeling now was normal; otherwise, they wouldn't be sending me home.

Michael packed my overnight bag and shoved my dirty underwear and unworn pajamas into the designer tote. I hadn't showered in over forty-eight hours and knew my hair was a greasy mess. I had tried to shower, but I got dizzy every time I stood up, so I gave up and stayed in bed. I hadn't puked since that first horrific night, and I thanked God for small miracles.

I asked the doctor about nausea and dizziness, fearful about the hour-long ride home and getting sick in between exits. The nurse gave me anti-nausea meds and reminded me to request them next time.

Next time. Why is there a next time?

I put on a brave face as Michael, the nurse, and I exited the building. Michael and the nurse chatted about the weather and football as I quietly tried to calm my mind. I was scared that I would accidentally do something stupid that would set me back.

Michael tried talking to me in the car, updating me on the kids, but I couldn't focus. My clammy hands, and rigid fingers curled amongst themselves in my lap. My leg wouldn't stop bouncing, and I pretended my excess movement was normal. The urge to pee was strong, but I knew it was just the anxiety of going home.

Michael kept asking random questions, and I tried my best to respond without extending the conversation. I wanted to get home, but I didn't want my kids to see me like this.

Instead, I focused on my eyes and my vision. I still couldn't read all the signs on the highway, and Michael's distorted face had a slight blur.

The past three days did nothing for me except cause physical pain and mental anguish.

When we got home, the kids sat around the kitchen island eating pizza. It was close to dinner time, and the sun had almost set.

Being in my house with my things and my family eased my mind. I waved to everyone and gave them hugs without getting too close.

I knew I smelled and my nostrils were twice as large as they were a few days before because of all the instruments shoved up the small holes for too many hours.

"I need to rest, but please come and say hi," I said to the kids.

Tiffany brought me a warm cup of ginger tea to soothe my stomach. She sat far away, so the couch cushions didn't shift under her weight. "How are you?" she asked.

I blew on the hot mug, feeling the warm steam rise around my chin, lips, and mouth. I shrugged my shoulders, feeling the hot tears form behind my eyes. "They didn't get it. They have to go in again." I think she already knew, but I could see the sadness in her eyes.

She grabbed my foot and squeezed. "I'll be here for you next time too. Don't worry. Anything you need, I'll be here."

I smiled, readjusted the chenille pillow, and closed my eyes.

"Hey, mom?" I heard a quiet voice near me. I opened my eyes and saw a blurry image of Robbie, standing at the edge of the couch.

"Hey, honey. Do you want to sit with me?"

Chapter 13

Robbie sat on the other side of the sectional, knowing not to get too close. "I'm happy you're home," he said.

"Thanks, honey. Me too. I have to have another surgery." I pursed my lips, swallowing the tremble.

"I missed you," he said, and then he was gone.

Alex didn't approach me until the next day. Still exhausted, but by then, no longer dizzy or nauseous, I took my physical progress as a win. My throat still burned, but I could get down soup, tea, and soupy mashed potatoes. I showered with Tiffany standing on the other side of the door, just in case I fell. She helped me get dressed to make sure I didn't bend at all.

Alex was a quiet girl who observed everything. She loved to play and loved people but never wanted to be the center of attention. She was happy with herself and was perfectly happy to play alone. She rarely showed affection. Hugging and kissing were not her favorite, but she showed her love by drawing a picture or making gifts. She was a beautiful person who was more reserved and cautious, which some people who didn't know her interpreted as rudeness.

I wasn't surprised that she didn't want to be near me, and I wasn't upset by it. I wanted her to come to me when she was ready. I knew that she had a closer relationship with Michael because she spent more time with him, so I reminded him to continue to check in with her feelings and thoughts.

The next three days were a complete blur. I traveled from my bed to the couch and back again. My sinus cavity had dried and crusted, making it difficult to breathe. I had purchased a nasal rinse to moisten my sinuses and hopefully clear up some of the dried blood from surgery. I wasn't allowed to sneeze or blow my nose for three weeks for fear of causing a cerebrospinal fluid leak, so the nasal rinse was my only relief. It wasn't doing anything to help ease my discomfort.

Tiffany had to go home. As I approached my second week of recovery, I tried to wrap my head around going back to work. Although I was improving every day, I still needed someone to stay with me. Michael would return to work, and Jessica would take a few days off from teaching to make me soup and help me shower. Michael was in charge of the kids and getting them to and from school, just like he always did.

For the first three days at home, I felt like my eyes were deteriorating. Everything was dark. I tried to read a bedtime story to Alex and failed miserably. The text disappeared into the page, and I needed a flashlight shining on the paper to see the letters. Alex gave up on me and stomped into the kitchen, asking Michael if he could finish the book because "Mom can't read."

When I looked at the microwave, the only numbers I deciphered were the minutes. When I looked at the dishwasher, I could only see the power light, even though the clean light shone brightly next to it. When I looked at myself in the mirror, the entire left side of my face looked like it was running down to my shoulder, without any clarity of facial features. My eyes seemed worse now than before the doctor poked and prodded my brain.

Tiffany told me to call my doctor if I was concerned, so I did. She told me to come back to the hospital to get a CT scan to ensure there wasn't an issue with the tumor itself. She told me she would notify the on-call neurologist and alert them that I was coming.

I thought I would arrive and immediately see the doctor. Michael and I debated whether we should go because I didn't want to go back. I was afraid something was seriously wrong, and I didn't want to be admitted again.

Tiffany said she would be heading home the following day, so if we were going to go, she could take care of Robbie and Alex. Michael and I climbed into the car for the familiar drive into Boston. I lay back in the captain's chair of the car with my eyes closed, focusing on the music emanating softly from the radio.

The Emergency Room was not that crowded, but no one had any idea they were expecting me, which was the impression I got when I spoke with the doctor. We went through the whole intake process to sit in a room and wait. After three hours of retelling my story repeatedly, we finally got to a room to speak to a doctor.

When I told the nurses Dr. Walker was expecting us, they responded, "This is an Emergency Department. We don't take reservations," or "I don't know who Dr. Walker is," or "There is no note of that here." With every retelling, I

Chapter 13

could feel my blood pressure rise and my patience diminish.

Finally, a young man, who introduced himself as part of the Neurology team, came in and said he had spoken to Dr. Walker. Based on her recommendations, we were going to have an MRI completed to rule out bleeding. He said it was unlikely due to the small amount of tumor removed, but it was better to be safe than sorry.

More hours ticked by. Going into the MRI machine was easy this time. I lay on my back, wondering if lying flat was doing me more harm than good. They had told me in the hospital that I needed to remain upright during my recovery because the pressure change in my head from lying horizontally could trigger a cerebrospinal fluid leak. I lay on the plank and trusted that they knew what they were doing.

I listened to the Congo drums bang in my ears and sang songs that matched the beat of the drum. I held onto the bulbous ball, ready to squeeze if I needed them to stop. At this point, I had already had seven MRIs and could almost guess when the scan was over. When the contrast went in, I knew I only had a few more pictures left.

A few hours later, the doctor approached me in the waiting room. There were people scattered around the room. Some sat in clothes, others in johnnies, some in wheelchairs, and others with nurses by their sides. He told me that the MRI looked good, and nothing concerning showed.

"Would you like a steroid to help reduce inflammation caused by surgery?" he asked.

I wasn't a doctor, but if he was suggesting it, why not?

Michael and I went into another room with a nurse, who injected me with Dexamethasone. I felt deep pins and needles run down my neck, across my shoulders, down my arms and torso, and into my legs within seconds. I felt like I was getting electrocuted and I asked the nurse if that was normal.

She nodded.

I looked over at Michael, and I could see every feature of his face. I saw both of his eyes, the angle of his nose, and the shape of his lips. It no longer looked like I was seeing him through a television set from 1985. He was three-dimensional and crisp.

"I can see!" I looked at the clock on the hospital wall, and saw the minutes hand clicking up to twelve. "I can see!" I said again, looking at Michael's face. "Thank you," I said to the nurse. She ushered us back out to the waiting room for our discharge papers.

Michael had an enormous smile across his face, and he squeezed my hand as if to say, 'We got this.' I sat there, in awe, looking around the waiting room. I could see the football game score on the television, read the ticker that ran under the score, and even read the signs on the walls.

The doctor came over to check on us, and I exclaimed that the steroids worked within seconds. He seemed surprised and a bit skeptical, but I knew what I saw now and what I saw before. He gave me a prescription for the steroids and told me Dr. Walker would call with the new surgery date.

I could have let that terrible reminder affect me, but I didn't care. The surgery wasn't happening now, and I could see. I couldn't wait to go home.

On the drive home, I read license plates out loud for the entire hour. I read highway signs and counted cars ahead of me. I hadn't been able to see for a long time, and I had been compensating for it with extra lights, larger font, and white duct tape. I had hope that if I could see this good now, with just a little medication, I would be able to see on my own, eventually.

That night I fell asleep in my own bed and breathed in the clean sheets that Michael had changed for me. Finally, I was home.

Chapter 14

"But, Michael…January tenth? I can't wait until January tenth. That is almost a month away," I said. "I need to go back to work at some point. I have to work…what are we going to do?" Exasperated by the lack of control I had over this situation, I threw the mail on the counter.

"Ashley, you have no choice. Did you ask Dr. Walker why?"

"Of course I did. She said scheduling was nearly impossible because three doctors needed to be present at the surgery. They teach, and they all teach on different days, and they aren't able to miss their classes. She said that they needed to schedule an eight am surgery so I was first. January tenth was the first available day."

Michael placed his hands on my shoulders and squeezed. "Then I guess it's January tenth," he responded.

The kids worked on their homework upstairs, and Michael and I warmed up dinner. The number of casseroles and meals dropped off by people in our community overwhelmed our refrigerator and freezer. Everyone at the kids' school knew about my surgery, and Jessica planned a meal train to help us recover. Meals overflowed from our fridge.

Grateful for the kindness of strangers, my mind couldn't help but turn to our finances. With the help of others, we saved on food costs, but where else could we save? I was out of work for the foreseeable future, and we needed to save where we could.

For dinner, we cooked chili and homemade bread. It looked delicious, and I could faintly smell the spices. I knew the kids wouldn't eat chili, but at least Michael and I had a few meals ready for us. Not only were people dropping off food, but also dropping off gift cards to grocery stores and restaurants.

Accepting their gifts was difficult for me, because there were times when people we knew needed assistance, and we had never donated. Half of the time, I was too distracted with our life to think about theirs. I always thought about the person and the situation when I heard the bad news, but never contributed. Now, knowing that I would only get 60% of my pay through short-term disability, I was blown away by their generosity and love.

"Who made the chili?" Michael asked.

"It's from the art teacher at the kids' school. I don't know her, but I'll send her a thank you card when everything is said and done."

Michael jotted her name in the notebook we kept for thank you cards.

"What are we doing about Christmas?" I changed the subject. "Christmas is in less than a week, and we haven't done anything." I rattled off the things we usually did but hadn't even started planning yet.

"Well," Michael said, "We aren't going to do it this year."

I dropped my spoon into my chili bowl and stared at him. *Could that be the answer?*

"We're not?" I asked him. "But we always do! What are people going to think if we cancel?"

I started to feel out of control again. The kids deserved a semi-normal Christmas, so we should do everything to make it happen. I couldn't physically do a lot of it, so to make it happen meant that someone else would be doing the work while I supervised and barked orders. I could see how it seemed a little unfair to Michael.

"Ashley, we're going to tell them that you have a brain tumor, and we'll try again next year. It is what it is." He scooped out another bowl of chili. "This is delicious."

I couldn't believe Michael was so nonchalant about dropping out of our yearly responsibilities. It wasn't just the parties but the moments with the kids that would also be eliminated. We needed to decorate the outside of

Chapter 14

the house and bake cookies, and send Christmas cards.

I shut my mouth and waited for my emotions to wash over me. I took a deep breath and pushed the air out of my nose. Michael was right. There was nothing I could do, and I couldn't put my expectations on others. I had to let it go.

It wasn't just shirking my responsibilities at home; it was knowing that my absence was disappointing others, as well. Jessica had been running the Girl Scout troop without me since my diagnosis. She said she didn't mind, but I knew how stressful the holidays were, and when you lose a significant helper, forget it. I felt like maybe if I tried harder to get back to normal, I could still be there for her to assist with all the projects.

"Okay," I started, replaying our conversation through my mind. "I think the one thing we must do is bake cookies together and visit Santa and Mrs. Claus." There I go again, trying to control the holiday and force fun on the family. "But other than that, nothing." I swallowed my pride and expectations and continued, "The kids are old enough to understand that life is different this year."

Michael nodded.

The kids knew things were different because I needed help doing everything. I couldn't bend over to empty the dishwasher, I couldn't lift a casserole dish to cook dinner in the oven, and I couldn't shower without the help of Michael. I couldn't drive them anywhere, and I couldn't read to Alex. Everything was in Michael's hands to help. I knew he was getting burned out, and I tried to call on Jessica as often as I could without burning her out, too.

Every few days for the first two weeks, I went to the hospital to get lab work done. They checked my cortisol level and sodium level to make sure that I wasn't dropping or developing diabetes insipidus. Every few days, I trekked into the local hospital and put out my arm for yet more blood draws.

At this point, it was second nature and didn't hurt at all. It became routine, and I learned which phlebotomists were true artists at their job. One phlebotomist injected the needle, drew the blood, and removed the needle before I had an opportunity to wince my eyes or furrow my brows.

My headaches still occurred, but the severity had lessened. No longer did a headache throw me on the bed in the dark with my eyes closed for the entire day. Instead, it was a dull, constant ache behind my eyes and right between my eyebrows. The miraculous steroid from the hospital had weaned out of my system, and as each day passed, I noticed a darker overtone and gentler lines to the left side of my sight. I honestly didn't know if I could go on like this. January tenth was too far away.

***

I begrudgingly went onto Amazon searching for Christmas gifts. Christmas Eve was four days away, and I knew it was close. It wasn't just the kids that needed a happy Christmas, but also the family members we see every Christmas Eve.

Every year we go to Rhode Island for Christmas Eve dinner and exchange gifts at Michael's parents. There was only one year we didn't make it since the kids were born, and that was due to a Nor'easter that dropped a foot of snow.

In November, I completed a Christmas list for the school and had no idea what gifts were purchased. The kids didn't need anything, and the things they wanted were out of our current price range.

Online, I ordered safe items that they would maybe love and probably like. Music for Robbie, stuffed animals for Alexandria, gift cards, and Lego sets. I checked the subtotal and wrote it down on our budgeting list. Done.

I had Robbie and Alex pick out toys for their cousins and purchased gift cards for their aunts and uncles. Generic gifts, sure, but I had other things concerning me.

I closed the laptop screen and scooped leftover beef stew into bowls, and placed fish sticks and macaroni and cheese on a plate for the kids.

The four of us sat down at the table. "I talked to my doctor today," I said, looking at Alexandria and Robbie. "I have to have another surgery. January tenth."

Both kids nodded.

"Is it going to be the same as last time?" Robbie asked.

I shrugged. "I don't know. There will be three doctors instead of two, and

Chapter 14

they are hoping to get the tumor out."

"Mom, will you be able to read to me again?" Alex asked.

"I hope so. And I hope to drive again. And work again. And get back to our lives again."

Alex took a bite to eat, accepting my answer.

"How long have you had it?" Robbie asked.

"The tumor? I don't know. Probably my whole life. They said it is growing slowly," I responded.

Michael started laughing. "Should we name it?"

"I know, right? This thing has been with me for way too long. It's practically part of the family. Hey," I said, glancing at Michael, "I said I always wanted three kids, right?"

He grinned at my joke.

"What about Walter?" Alex suggested.

"No, Gregory," Robbie contributed.

"I kind of like Timmy," Michael added.

"Timmy the Tumor. I like it!" I confirmed. From that point forward, we talked about Timmy, the trouble he was causing us, and what we would do when Timmy got evicted. By naming the elephant in the room, it became less scary for the kids and me. All I wanted was for Timmy to go and my vision to return. That was my Christmas wish.

Chapter 15

Christmas was three days away. The kids finished their last day of school before the extended break, and a fresh layer of snow coated the ground. It was enough to look out the window and appreciate the beauty of the white fallen crystals but not enough to shovel or alter your plans to accommodate Mother Nature.

I felt okay. Not great, but not terrible. I started to feel more normal a week after my surgery. I could swallow again without any pain, talk at an average volume without having that smoker's rasp, and move about as I typically would. I still struggled with my sense of smell, so I baked cakes and cookies to stimulate my nose and keep me busy.

I hadn't been to work in over a month, and I didn't miss it. Of course, I missed the money, but while home, when everyone else was working or at school, I caught up on all the television I had missed over the years. I refused to feel guilty for not cleaning the house. The doctor's orders said no laundry, no dishwasher, no making the bed, and no leaning over, which meant no cleaning the bathroom. By having my doctor say no, I dismissed the guilt that hovered over me. I wanted to clean, but I couldn't. Our housecleaner came in every other week, which alleviated any stress within me.

Instead, I spent the day on the couch in my day pajamas watching television or in the kitchen baking. I probably shouldn't have lifted cake pans and muffin tins, but the doctor said no more than ten pounds, and although my

Chapter 15

baking wasn't great, the end product never weighed more than a dumbbell. Just in case, I bent at the knees to put the pans in and out of the lower oven.

Whenever I bent at the waist, my head throbbed and threatened to knock me down.

After the first few weeks of the Dexamethasone injection, I read to Alex, but eventually, my vision returned to baseline.

I appreciated this time off from work and time away from my family while they were at school. It allowed me to reflect on all that I had endured.

Television and movies were a good distraction because I never paid that much attention to what was happening. I completed puzzles because I wanted to challenge my eyes. I knitted, which was something I enjoyed as a little girl but hadn't done in years. I painted, partly because I was bored and partly because I wanted to challenge my interpretation of color.

Even though Christmas was fast approaching, I tried not to stress over it. We ordered what we could afford off of Amazon and had picked up the donations from the school. Beyond blessed by the generosity of their teachers and the town, we knew that even if the kids didn't get everything on their list, they got enough to keep them occupied and entertained.

Accepting black trash bag after black trash bag filled with wrapped gifts almost felt like stealing, but I pushed it aside because we didn't know what my future held. For all I knew, I may never work again. We decided to accept the generosity with a thankful heart and vowed to pay it forward when I was medically cleared.

I did as much as I could while the kids attended school. My house cleaner was also my holiday helper, and she wrapped the remaining gifts, went shopping for the Christmas Eve platter and Christmas Day meal, and decorated the house with the plethora of fake trees sitting in storage.

Even though Michael and I had discussed eliminating all unnecessary Christmas traditions, I sneaked in a few extra tasks without him looking. Maybe he wouldn't even notice. I was the master juggler and I always got it done.

On their last day of school, the kids and I transformed the house into a winter wonderland. Robbie decorated the fireplace with white garland and

Christmas houses, and stockings hung on the sterling silver bell holders and tree holders from Tiffany's.

These new additions completed the house, magnificently enhancing the trees that already twinkled with lights. I looked around and smiled in satisfaction. From an outsider looking in, it appeared that we had it all together. I wondered when Michael would notice.

The next few days were an excitement of Christmas desire. The kids helped prepare the Christmas cookies and bread for the neighbors and our church pastor, and they went through their clothes and toys in their bedrooms to make room for what was coming. Alex had an elf, Thomas, who visited before Christmas to watch over her and report back to Santa Claus. Thomas told us that Santa would collect our donations when he delivered his gifts Christmas morning. This year, the kids filled boxes with clothes, toys, books, and stuffed animals. It was an excellent way to give back to those who needed it and clear out the clutter in our house.

Christmas Eve morning, we woke up to more than just a coating of snow on the ground. The temperature had been hovering around freezing all week, and any time snow was in the forecast, freezing rain and sleet came first.

I sat at the table with Michael, holding a piping hot mug of tea. "Hey, Michael? Do you think you can shovel before the temperature comes up again and turns the snow back to freezing rain?" I knew I couldn't lift a shovel, let alone a shovel full of wet, heavy snow. "Robbie can help you."

Michael nodded. "I have some last-minute shopping before we head to my parents. I'll go out in a little bit."

I smiled a small smile because it was just like him to be unprepared on Christmas Eve. I knew that his shopping endeavor was for me, and he would probably come home with whatever was picked over and left on the dressing room floor. Maybe it would be in my size or something I liked, but most likely, it wouldn't. Year after year, I tried on the too big sweater or bucket handbag with too many pockets or jacket that just barely buttoned when I stood naked underneath. Christmas gifts for me became a running joke in this family on just how bad Michael's fashion taste was. Every year I

Chapter 15

returned at least one of his gifts for something I liked.

"Oh boy," I joked. "I can't wait to see what you come home with this year!" I winked at him and took a sip of my tea, not quite breaking eye contact.

That afternoon, lying on the couch, watching a Christmas movie, I heard a crash and felt the house shake.

Alex ran into the room. "Mom! What was that?"

Robbie entered the house covered in snow and holding the mail in his glove.

"Robbie, what was that? Are you okay?"

"Yeah. What was that?" Robbie looked outside. "I don't see anything." He took off his wet gloves and threw them on the kitchen counter, bunched into a ball.

I threw on my slippers and stepped out the front door, careful to avoid any ice. I turned to our driveway and looked down the hill. "Michael!"

Flat on his back like a pancake, he stared into the sky. I tried to get to him but it was too risky with the ice. Scanning the driveway, I saw a sheet of thick, white ice, except for at the very top. At the bottom of the hill, the car wedged itself into the side of our attached garage, just beyond where Michael lay.

I tried to run to Michael, but my lack of tread immediately made me lose my balance. As I caught myself, fear consumed me as I pictured an alternate reality of me falling on the ice, hitting my head, and causing more damage to my brain. I stood where I was, unable to move, and called out to Michael.

Robbie and Alex stood behind me, Alex's hand cupped over her mouth.

"What happened?" I asked Robbie again.

Michael rolled onto all fours and crawled across the driveway.

"I don't know," Robbie said. "Dad, are you okay?" He turned back to me without waiting for an answer. "We were done shoveling the top. Dad told me to go inside because he was going shopping for a few hours."

I sat on the ground and slowly slid myself to Michael while listening to Robbie explain the sequence of events. Michael, although moving, stayed silent. His eyes widened with terror, and his hands shook.

"Are you okay?" I called to him, my pants saturated and my butt numb.

"The car," he cried. Mumbling in gibberish, I couldn't make out any of the words. Once I got to him, I placed my hands on his shoulders, and stared into his eyes.

"It's okay. It's okay. It's okay. The car doesn't matter. What matters is you. Are you okay?" I asked.

Michael continued to nod at me, unable to meet my eyes. The stricken horror set deeper in the fine lines around his eyes and mouth.

"I'm so sorry," he said.

We crawled down to the bottom of the driveway, silent as we passed the car that cost too much money, and entered the house through the back door.

"Michael. It's a car," I said. "It's a car, and it doesn't matter. I can't even drive right now. We don't need two cars. All I care about is that you are okay. What happened?"

Michael couldn't get his thoughts together, but the keywords he had given me were "car…trunk…ice…stop".

"You tried to stop the car?" Alex translated. She stood in the three-season porch attached to our garage.

Michael nodded.

"You could have been killed!" I imagined Michael grabbing onto the rear bumper, trying to stop a car from traveling down an icy ski slope. That must have been how he ended up in the middle of the driveway.

"I was going to go to the store. I got in the car. I realized my boots were soaking wet, and I got out of the car to change my shoes. The next thing I know, the car is rolling down the driveway. I tried to stop it, but I couldn't," he explained.

I wrapped my arms around him and buried my face in his cold shoulder from the wet driveway. "It's okay. It's just a car. You're okay. We'll call the insurance company, have the garage checked out. It's fine. I'm not working and have nothing else to do. We're all home for Christmas break. It's going to be okay." I reassured him with every positive thought I could muster.

The car stayed wedged into the front corner of the garage for the next three days because it was Christmas and our accident wasn't a priority. We couldn't leave the house until the tow truck removed the car, and it blocked

Chapter 15

our driveway, preventing our other car from leaving.

The kids had to adjust, yet again, to a new Christmas experience. It looked like Rhode Island, and visiting family was not happening this year.

On Christmas morning, I woke up to find a beautiful handmade card from Michael with a gift card to Amazon inside. I knew the gift card had come with all the kids' school donations, and I smiled at him for his effort. Perhaps next year would be different.

Chapter 16

Round two of surgery was the same as round one. Tiffany came up to spend the week with the kids, and Jessica took over for any additional needs until I recovered. Hank and Janet volunteered on weekends, and Amanda and Jason did what they could to pitch in financially. I had been out of work for eight weeks, and my paid leave had expired the paycheck before. Not going to Christmas ended up being a financial blessing.

Michael and I headed out in our newly fixed Range Rover to Boston. The dark sky was the color of three-day-old bruises, and the horizon hadn't started its transition from black to orange to pink to blue. My packed hospital bag sat at my feet, and this time I threw in a few extra Chapstick tubes and headphones. I didn't think I could listen to music, but maybe by the end of my stay, the music could drown out the beeping of all the machines in the hospital room.

I spoke with my neurosurgeon the week before and reminded her that I needed anti-nausea meds, and the IV placed in my arm instead of my hand. "Please put it in my chart," I said, desperate for confirmation that I wouldn't be set on fire again.

She reassured me that things would go much smoother this time around, and with the expertise of another surgeon, she was hopeful and confident that I would leave the hospital a lighter woman free from Timmy. I took what she said with a grain of salt, refusing to get my hopes up for a flawless

Chapter 16

experience.

Michael placed his hand on my knee as we traveled down the Pike. "How are you feeling?" He glanced at me.

"Scared," I responded.

"What are you worried about?"

I hesitated. So many worries swirled through my head. "What if they don't get it? What if I can never drive again? What if I can't work? How are the kids handling all of this? How are you handling this? What if I mentally can't do the surgery and the recovery again?" My fears spilled out like an overflowing jar of jelly beans. I worried every night in bed, waiting for my eyes to get so heavy, I'd fall asleep into nothingness.

It didn't help that I had been sleeping upright for the past few weeks on the couch. Michael's snoring kept me awake when I tried to sleep in the bed, and the angle of the pillows caused panic to set in that a cerebrospinal fluid leak would develop. Even though my sleep was terrible at best, I knew the couch would give me the freedom to turn on the television without waking a soul.

"It'll be okay." Michael, the forever optimist, made me smile. "This is a repeated road. The kids know what to expect. Tiffany was fine last time, and Dr. Walker is confident that she'll get Timmy out."

I looked at him and tried to put on a brave face, but I could feel the lump in my throat grow. As the signage for Boston became more and more frequent, my anxiety rose deep within me.

"You'll be fine. You'll wake up, and I will be there. Recovery is going to suck, but you did it before. It's going to be a week of hell, but we will get through it together."

By the time we got to the hospital, the sky had started to turn a light shade of gray. It looked like it wanted to snow, and it smelled like snow, but there was no snow in the forecast. I was thankful that the weather would be decent for the next week. Another snow storm was the last thing we needed.

"Here," I said to Michael, shoving a piece of folded paper into his hand.

"What's this?" he asked, unfolding the paper.

"My final wishes. I know I shouldn't worry, but this is a big deal. It isn't every day that someone probes your brain and takes part of it out." I looked at my hands, fumbling with my cell phone. "I know last time was not what we expected, and I would hate to have something happen this time and not be prepared." I dropped my phone into my purse and smiled up at him.

The document, although not official, was quickly written before I fell asleep the night before. I kept thinking about my parents and how they unexpectedly left me on a chilly day in November. A quick trip to the store ended with a car crash and a finality I still struggled to process.

When I was fourteen, my parents left us to go out to dinner. Jason and I sat on our old, plaid sofa with wooden arms in our basement watching The Real World when our dog, Frankie, started barking. We ignored her and turned up the television. The dog never stopped barking. Jason thought maybe Mom and Dad had forgotten their house keys or had their hands full and couldn't maneuver the door handle, so he answered it.

He returned to me with pale, white, empty eyes and stiff movements. He sat down next to me, and I saw a police officer hide in the shadows of the basement stairs. I gave him a look and muted the television. "You okay?" I asked, glancing from Jason to the cop to Jason again.

The police officer made his way over to me and said, "You need to come to the station. There's been an accident."

Our parents thought they were invincible and they were our heroes. They weren't organized, but always figured it out, whether it was how to pay the bills, send us to camp, or create a fantastic birthday party on a budget.

What they didn't have was a will, and Jason and I were both minors. Our grandparents were issued guardianship after a lengthy legal battle with the state.

I don't remember anything after that except that we moved halfway across the state into our grandparents' home. I was a freshman, and Jason was a senior. Our lives flipped upside down.

Prior to the accident, we had a close relationship with our grandparents and saw them multiple times a year, but they were old. They were in their 70s and hadn't had to raise teenagers in over forty years. Jason and I struggled with their rules and expectations during that transition.

Chapter 16

Jason and I brought our clothes and a handful of personal items to their house. We stayed in the extra bedrooms with generic furniture and linens. All of our other belongings stayed in storage until Jason and I were old enough to use it for our first apartments.

When Jason moved out, I was devastated all over again. First, I lost my parents, friends, school, and life, and then I lost my lifeline to normalcy. Those two years without him while I finished high school was most difficult. I didn't have any friends. My grandparents tried, but they didn't understand me, and every day I went through the motions.

Every holiday, birthday, and activity I had shared with my parents took me years to get through in one piece.

When I found out I was pregnant with Robbie, I didn't know if I was ready to be responsible for another person. What would happen if I left him unexpectedly to get through life alone?

Although I would never admit it to Michael, I needed to provide Robbie with support to get through hard times when Michael and I weren't available. That was the reason why I wanted another baby so badly. I was afraid I would eventually abandon them as my parents did to me. My greatest gift to Robbie was Alex.

Michael placed his hand on my knee, and my eyes returned to him. He scanned the handwritten document, and I watched his face contort and his hand shake. "Okay. I'm tucking this away for safe keeping because we aren't going to need it."

I nodded and smiled. Grateful we weren't going to talk about the letter's contents, I wasn't emotionally strong enough to imagine the pain my departure would cause my children.

In the hospital, we went through the same process again. We sat in the outpatient surgery room, got our restaurant beeper, followed the nurse into the makeshift waiting room, waited for transport, and headed off to the Operating Room. It was a little after seven in the morning when we got to the OR waiting room, and all the doctors scurried in to review the plan.

Michael was with me this time, and he heard firsthand all the risks associated with my surgery.

"We'll call you in a few hours with an update. We expect it will be a few hours," Dr. Walker told him.

With that, Michael and I parted ways with a hand squeeze and a kiss, and I didn't see him again until I awoke from the anesthesia.

The next thing I remember, the sun was up, and I couldn't breathe. I tried to open my eyes, but the light was too strong and it blinded me. Pain beamed through my eyes and I kept them closed. Grateful, nausea and dizziness hadn't returned.

The first few nights, my dreams consisted of strobe light dance parties. Someone stood behind my closed eyelids, shining flashlights out of both eyes. When my eyes were closed, I couldn't tell if it was day or night because my eyelids lit up like firecrackers.

The nurse told me Michael was in and out of my ICU room those first few days, but I didn't remember. I slept most of the day and night, except for waking up for my meds. The neuro team periodically stopped in to check my vision. Fingers waved above and below my face, flashlights dilated my pupils, and a handheld eye chart on someone's cell phone accompanied every check-in.

I noticed that my right forearm in the crease of my elbow was black, blue, and purple, and the IV port was on my other arm. I knew when the anesthesiologist poked me that it wasn't going to end well. She flicked my arm and pressed on my vein to make it pop. I flinched at her touch, averting my eyes away from the needle.

A nurse entered my room to give me my meds and draw labs. "Hi," she said, smiling. "How are you feeling?"

"Okay. Would you mind turning off the light?" She showed me how to control the lights and bed positioning from the bedside panel and clicked the button until the room dimmed.

"You'll be heading to the Neuro floor shortly. We're waiting for a room to open. How is your pain?"

"Like a four. I can't breathe, and I feel really out of it."

"Yeah, you have packing in your nose. You're going to have to breathe through your mouth. Make sure you drink water or chew on ice, and

Chapter 16

remember, no straws," she reiterated.

I didn't know what packing was. I pulled out my cell phone to see my reflection, and a giant cotton swab hanging out both nostrils greeted me. It looked like they were tied together with dental floss. They were black and wet, and my nostrils were twice as wide as their typical size. I touched it and felt the moisture seep out under my nose and above my upper lip. My face looked puffy, and the purple bags under my eyes protruded beyond my cheek bones.

I barely recognized myself. This was not what I expected or how it was the first time. My face looked like it had been smashed in by a shovel.

I slept the week away, both in the hospital and at home, and each day bled into the next. Tiffany was at our house for a few days and made sure I had food and drinks to satisfy my hunger. Michael gave me my medications around the clock. I was on many more drugs this recovery period, and they all required a different schedule. Anti-seizure meds, antibiotics, steroids, thyroid meds, pain relievers; I couldn't keep it straight. Just looking at the pill box caused me anxiety, and when I tried to be responsible for my medication, my mind was a jumbled mess. It was safer if I wasn't accountable.

The kids freaked out, especially Alex. She wouldn't come near me because I had the packing hanging out of my nose, and it was first wet, bloody, and squishy and then longer, black, and rigid. I couldn't do any nasal rinses until the ENT pulled out the packing ten days after my surgery.

Alex was afraid of me, but my brain was mush, so I couldn't deal with her discomfort even if I wanted to. Instead, I retreated to my room as I slowly regained strength and my brain fog diminished.

That second week, Jessica stayed with me so Michael could go back to work. I felt less like a zombie but still hadn't showered in days. I tried to shower, but I lost my balance in the hot, steamy air. By leaning forward to pick up the body wash, the elevation change triggered the pressure in my nose to shift, and I gasped at my stupidity. The doctor had repaired my sinus cavity with my abdominal fat, and until it healed I was at risk of it rupturing.

On my last day in the hospital, Dr. Walker had told me that the surgery was a success. She said that they removed two-thirds of the tumor, but it was still a challenging surgery. They started at eight in the morning and ended at midnight, slowly ripping apart the sticky tar that made up my tumor. She had difficulty breaking it up into small enough pieces to fit through the suction tube.

She told me they removed enough to relieve the pressure from my optic nerve, so my vision should be returning. Although the tumor sat a few millimeters away from my nerve, it had started pulsing in surgery. Blood was finally flowing to my eyes.

I couldn't believe it. I felt like I was in a dream, and this was happening to someone else.

All the specialists came in to talk about the success of the surgery, but I couldn't comprehend. They might have told me leprechauns and unicorns had taken over the world, and I would have believed them.

There had been a small leak during surgery, which is why they had to patch up the hole, but because of the shape of the tumor that remained, the patch was slightly haphazard and needed to be monitored. The risk of a leak post-surgery was higher than what they expected.

Endocrinology took more blood, and I had a follow-up appointment for my eyes a few weeks later.

My cortisol and estrogen levels dropped, and my thyroid was borderline and steadily decreasing over time. I had just entered the phase of my life where I needed daily medication to survive and function. I knew when I got home that I would be running to the local hospital every other day to get my numbers checked. To make the experience more humiliating, two bloody tampons hung from my nose, so I covered them with gauze.

It seemed like all the doctors and specialists were impressed with my tumor. The sheer size and consistency were atypical. The number of hours it took to remove it and how it affected my hormones was also odd. The doctors collected my tumor and sent it to the research bank to help others who would struggle with my same diagnosis in the future.

"Hey Ashley," Jessica whispered as I slowly opened my eyes. The light was so bright. I searched for my sunglasses. "Here is some chicken noodle soup. I thought the broth might help."

Chapter 16

The packing drove me crazy. Fluid pushed out the wet gauze every time I swallowed and created tiny bubbles under my nostrils and above my lips. I had learned that when I swallowed, I needed to take tiny sips because the more significant, the greater the pressure increased, and the more fluid would seep out my nose. My ears popped occasionally, and I silently worried about getting a perforated ear drum. I needed to get this out.

I needed fluids at all times because the packing dried out my oral cavity and my tongue felt like sandpaper. Just moving my tongue caused me to gag because everything rubbed against each other like the bristles of a grill brush running across a rusty grill.

I continued to sleep upright with my mouth open because I couldn't breathe when I closed my mouth. I had never felt so uncomfortable, and between the headaches, light sensitivity, and dry mouth, my brain couldn't process anything.

I took the bowl of soup from her and nursed the warm broth, ignoring the messiness of my experience. I wiped my nose, which remained wet and soggier as the days increased, and took a few bites before I caught my breath. "Thank you. This is amazing." I said, sounding like I had a cold.

"You're doing great," she said. "You are so strong and brave." She squeezed my arm, and I nodded toward her with my eyes closed.

I lay in bed for over a week. Sleep was interrupted to take my medications, and I played music to pass the time. My eyes couldn't process television and reading was off limits. In and out of consciousness, I thought about what I went through and what I was experiencing.

I had no idea why this had happened to me, and from what I understood, it was completely random. There was no known cause, and they suspected it had been growing for years, so the why was irrelevant. The reality was that I had this, and not only did I have to deal with it, but so did my family. Alex was frightened, Robbie was cautious, and Michael had been an angel, floating in to take care of me when I was too out of it to notice.

I remembered the first time I had met Michael, my freshman year at college. We worked in a library because I loved reading and learning, and he loved hanging out. Libraries weren't often busy, so it was a no-stress job. We worked in the microfiche department, which no longer exists.

If you asked college kids today to find the research articles they need in the microfiche department, they might look at you like you had three heads. Micro-what? Michael and I worked there before the internet ruled the world and would give you all the information and misinformation you might not need.

From the moment I met Michael, his kindness overwhelmed me. He wasn't concerned about being the cool kid or being invited to all the parties. He seemed comfortable with himself and confident in who he was and what he believed. We would sit behind the microfiche desk, with all my textbooks and notebooks spread out on the table, and Michael, with no work, leaned back in his chair observing things and people around us.

I had a boyfriend at the time, so we were strictly just friends that sometimes had lunch together. I trusted him from the moment I met him. I didn't understand why I felt pulled to him or how I felt so safe when I was around him. I think it was because he was never a threat to me. I never had to worry that he would try and get me drunk and take advantage of me or that he would use me for a night of fun and then discard me. He always respected the fact that I had a boyfriend, which made me more drawn to him.

And then, a few years later, I found myself single, wondering what had happened to Michael. I had left college and returned home, and he had left as well. All I had was an email address and an AOL instant messenger screen name. I thought of him often and hoped that he was doing well.

Three years after that first encounter at work, we reconnected. So much life had been lived by both of us during those years away from each other.

One day, in the middle of a snowstorm in January, I drove four hours to see him. I had stayed with him for the weekend, trusting that I wouldn't regret it. I trusted that he wouldn't take advantage of me or put me in an uncomfortable situation that would leave me sleeping in my car.

That night was the beginning of a long-distance courtship that allowed us to become closer friends and take things slow. After that night, we had a long-distance relationship, followed by multiple apartments, then a wedding, then Robbie, and then Alex. Life rapidly changed once we reconnected, but

Chapter 16

we always managed to go through the changes together.

If I had to go through this horrendous experience with someone, I was happy Michael was by my side.

I continued to lay in bed, unaware that Jessica was still sitting with me. "Hey, Jess?" I called out.

"I'm right here," she said, rubbing my foot.

"Will you help me shower and get dressed? I want to feel normal again."

Jessica supported me while I hobbled to the shower. The room rotated slightly, and the fatigue increased as I stepped out of my pajamas and into the shower.

Jessica stood outside the bathroom door. "I'm right here if you need me," she called through the door.

The hot water coated my body and burned away all the physical pain. The drumming of the water hitting the shower floor hypnotized my busy mind. I stared straight ahead because any movement of my neck and head caused the pressure to change in my sinuses. I stood like a statue and fumbled blindly for my shampoo and soap.

Washing my body without bending or twisting proved difficult, and I tried to clean my hair without tipping my head back. I still couldn't breathe, and the multi-tasking of moving and living exhausted me. I had no idea how long I stayed in there or how well I cleaned myself, but I finally felt like a human for the first time in over a week.

Chapter 17

"Okay, Ashley. You're going to feel a quick pull, but it will be over in a second." I looked at Dr. Scully and closed my eyes. I didn't know what he was doing to get these pads out of my head, and I didn't want to know. I felt pressure race through my nasal cavity, and then cool air hit me like a freight train. By the time I opened my eyes, the packing was already in the trash can.

"How do you feel?" he asked.

How do I feel? I can breathe again! I no longer had liquid dripping down my face onto my upper lip, and I felt and looked normal again. "So much better," I replied.

"Now, there is disposable packing up under your eyes, which should disintegrate by our next appointment," he explained. "If they are still there, we will remove them, but it should be fine."

Next, he stuck an endoscope up my nose to check the packing and clean out my sinuses. I closed my eyes. I didn't want to know what had been trapped in my nose for the past ten days. He pulled dried blood clots out of my nose, and when he finished, I could breathe like usual.

"Make sure you do nasal rinses every day," he said, handing me a squeeze bottle. "Be careful. We don't want a leak to erupt. I'll see you in three months."

Dr. Scully was my first follow-up appointment. I left his office feeling

Chapter 17

rejuvenated and hopeful. Being able to breathe through my nose and swallow without popping my ears was enough to make me giddy.

The next appointment I had was in a few weeks with the Neuro-Ophthalmologist. My vision was my biggest concern, and I was nervous but trying not to think about it.

My superpower, I had decided, was Super Sight. Instead of seeing everything like I was viewing a painting, I was now seeing a photograph. Driving into Boston, I knew every window, line, and color in the skyline across the Charles River. I saw the snow's vibrancy on the ground compared to the blue of the sky. The colors were lively and varied. I even found that I had to close my eyes when looking at pictures of sunsets because the colors were so bright. I stopped seeing flashlights and strobe light beams shining behind my eyelids when I tried to sleep, but I still needed to wear sunglasses both inside and outside the house.

My vision had never been better, but I anticipated the return to baseline once the steroids wore off. Just like last time.

"Hey Ash, I bought you a present," Michael said, pulling a small wrapped rectangle from his backpack.

"Thank you." I loved getting gifts unexpectedly.

I unwrapped the paper and held a beautiful gratitude journal in my hands. Each page was just large enough to write down one or two things that I was thankful for on that day. "Thank you, this is great." I kissed him, feeling the softness of his lips against mine.

"I know things have been kind of crappy lately, and I wanted you to know that I'm grateful for you and everything you've done for us over the years," Michael explained. "If you want, we can do this journal together as a family. It'll keep us connected because I know we're all struggling in our own way." His thoughtfulness was something I had always admired.

The kids came home from school that afternoon, and Alex gave me my first hug since before my second surgery. My heart melted when she approached me and wrapped her skinny arms around me.

"Hi, mom. How was your appointment?" she asked.

I was taken aback by her sudden ease around me. "It was great. The doctor said everything is healing well, and I am on track to be back to normal soon."

"I missed you," Alex said, hugging me again. "Do you think you can read to me before bed tonight?"

I felt weak, but I needed to read her at least one chapter in her book.

"Absolutely." A renewed sense of motivation propelled me forward. I needed to be the mom my kids deserved.

I pulled out a frozen meal for dinner that night, dropped off by a neighbor. The amount of food flowing out of our fridge and freezer was both overwhelming and endearing. I had no idea so many people cared about us, and again, I told myself that I would write a thank you card to all of them.

"Did you hear about that weird virus?" Michael asked me.

I shook my head no. I hadn't turned on the news in months.

"Yeah, it's a contagious virus that started in China a few weeks ago. They went into lockdown because it's that contagious. I guess cases have been showing up throughout Europe too, but it is mostly in China," he explained.

"Huh. That's weird. I hope it isn't anything serious," I replied, not understanding the scope of what was to come.

"Did you talk to work?"

"I did. I can't go back until after I see Dr. Walker, and I can't drive until I see Dr. Chalksky, so I told them I would be out until the end of February at least." I replied.

"I think we need to sit down and look at our finances now that Christmas is over."

I nodded. I loved analyzing finances because numbers made sense to me. They could be manipulated in so many different ways and still end at the same spot.

Since my first surgery, I hadn't paid the bills because the brain fog stopped me clear in my tracks. "I'll sit down with you tomorrow so we can figure it out," I responded. We had considerable savings in place, so I wasn't worried yet, but knew that if I didn't return to work soon, our savings would dwindle to a place that made me uneasy.

That night we looked closely at what we were bringing in and what we

Chapter 17

were putting out. Since December, people had been feeding us and dropping off gift cards to restaurants and grocery stores. I knew I would be out of work for a while longer, but the hope was that I would be back full-time by March.

The kids received free lunch and complimentary breakfast whenever they wanted. Our grocery bill had been essentially a tenth of what we usually spent. Michael and I decided that we would buckle down and only go grocery shopping every few weeks. That would make us use what we had and get creative.

We cut out Robbie's music lessons and Alexandria's dance classes because the cost was astronomical. We tried only to impact the kids when all other options had been exhausted.

As February vacation approached, I felt great. Even though the doctor hadn't cleared me, I drove around town, running errands while everyone else was at work and school. I cooked meals, kept the house in order, and purged boxes of stuff that had been accumulating since we bought our house eight years before. I had to rest every day from the fatigue of it all, but my overall energy level was growing daily.

We booked a trip to the White Mountains in New Hampshire for a few days during February vacation. From a financial standpoint, Michael and I knew it was foolish, but we felt the kids deserved a break from our stressful lives.

The kids had stumbled through school, dealing with questions from their teacher, and questions from their friends. I pictured Alex's stiff posture when her friends asked why she couldn't have play dates the way she had before, or Robbie's nonchalance when the teachers asked how I was.

Michael and I thought that if we could take the kids away for a few days, we would celebrate the success of the surgeries and the return to more typical life.

The day before our trip, Alexandria woke up complaining of stomach pain. She lounged on the couch, watching a movie. We gave her some ginger ale, which was an upset stomach remedy that my parents gave me when I was a kid. A few hours later, she couldn't keep anything down. She vomited water and didn't have an appetite for food. Concerned with dehydration, I debated if I should call the doctor.

Her low-grade fever increased to a fully developed fever. The fever-reducing medications we gave her lasted in her belly for less than ten minutes before she vomited again.

As she lay on the floor in the fetal position, her eyes stared blankly and sideways at the television. The color in her face was ashen, and the skin around her eyes swelled. Michael was a proponent of letting the virus get out of her system with time, but we had a vacation to get to, and I couldn't let a stomach bug stop us.

I called the pediatrician asking if we could do anything to assist with her recovery or help her fever drop. The nurse said that if she was still vomiting around dinner time, we should take her to the closest Urgent Care. She noted that Alex might need fluids.

"It's cheaper and faster to do it at Urgent Care than at the Emergency Room," the nurse said.

I pulled Michael into our bedroom. "They want her to go to Urgent Care if she doesn't get better." I looked at my watch. "Do you think we should?" We considered the co-pay and the wait.

Michael shrugged. "Let's see what happens."

I sat next to Alex and rubbed her head, feeling the heat emanate into my fingers. I kissed her on the forehead and placed a cold washcloth along the back of her neck.

Robbie came barreling down the stairs with a backpack pressed against his lower back. "I'm ready to go," he said. His guitar hung over his shoulder.

His image transported me ten years into the future. I pictured him as a rockstar packing up for a gig. His shaggy brown hair covered his eyes, and the black hooded sweatshirt, guitar, and backpack made him look much older than a mere eleven.

In my mind, the image transitioned to him at eighteen, leaving for college, and I blinked back tears. I couldn't understand why I was so emotional or so stricken by how old he looked. It seemed like I was seeing him for the first time in a long time.

Chapter 17

He was no longer the colicky infant who cried all hours of the night or the toddler who melted down with every overstimulated sensation. I remembered the kindergartner who held my hand on the first day of school as we walked up the steps, his little hand quivering.

He suddenly grew into a kind, loving young man. College was a few years away, but I saw him leaving us for good. I hoped when he looked back on his childhood, he saw a family that gave their all.

Right now, he was ready to get away from our current life and reset from all the stress, transitions, and forced flexibility. I saw who he had become while I was too busy working and then recovering to notice. Not only did a sense of pride wash over me, but also a layer of sadness. I couldn't understand how I had missed so much.

"Thank you for packing, Robbie. Your sister is still sick, so we might have to postpone our trip for a few days."

Michael and I booked the mountain home for an entire week despite only staying two nights. Even though it cost twice as much money, we knew that my recovery could influence our trip, and we didn't want to lock ourselves into a date that we may not keep.

Robbie dropped his stuff at the door and headed into the kitchen for a snack. "Okay," he said, glancing at Alex, passed out on the floor. "I'm ready whenever you are."

That night, Robbie, Michael, and I ate dinner while Alex slept. She hadn't eaten anything, and she still couldn't keep liquids down.

We took her to Urgent Care and waited in the waiting room with sick children, adults in masks, and toddlers crying. My head started to throb from the stress of the day and the anticipation of our vacation.

A peppy, young nurse called us into the room. Her big smile and gentle eyes distracted us from the discomfort Alex was experiencing. As she checked Alex's vitals and asked about her symptoms, we told her about our pending vacation and how we hoped we could still go. She wished us luck and swapped places with the doctor.

The doctor poked and prodded Alex while asking her about school, winter activities, vacation plans, and Christmas. Every time she pressed Alex's side,

Alex would retract her leg and squirm uncomfortably on the table. The doctor ignored her movements and continued poking and prodding and asking questions.

Robbie, Michael, and I squeezed into the small room with the two of them, waiting for a diagnosis and prognosis.

"Well, I think she needs to get to the hospital," the doctor said, behind the cloth curtain separating us from our children. Michael and I looked at each other, not quite believing the amount of bad luck we had been blessed with over the past four months.

"Why?" I asked.

"Well, I think it is her appendix. The pain described is a typical pattern in children, and the touch response is also typical. They will see what is going on with an ultrasound. It is common," she explained.

I looked at my watch. It was almost eight at night.

"I will call the hospital to let them know you are coming," the doctor added.

I knew how that worked. It didn't speed up the process at all. I knew we would be there for most of the night.

When we climbed into the car to head to the local hospital, Robbie complained about how we probably wouldn't be able to go on vacation, and Alex cried in discomfort or fear, I wasn't sure. We sat in the main Emergency Room waiting area for hours, watching other families enter the E.R. before us. They finally called us just before midnight.

The ultrasound was inconclusive, but it had all the classic indicators. Because the technician couldn't get a clear picture, she wouldn't make a diagnosis, and the hospital couldn't admit Alex without a diagnosis.

Instead, the four of us crammed into a tiny room with a single hospital bed for Alex, and three chairs for us. The nurse and doctors told us that Alex was on the surgery list for the next day because they believed she had appendicitis but they needed a clear image to make it official.

Throughout the night and early morning, we chatted amicably with the staff. We explained the hell we had been living through for the previous four months. The next thing we knew, the hospital had brought in a second bed for me to lay in next to Alex so my head would remain elevated. Robbie

Chapter 17

slept on two seats of regular plastic chairs positioned to create a bench, and Michael slept in a backward folding chair. His arms draped across the top of the chair's back, and his head rested on his arms.

At three in the morning, Alex woke for a CAT-SCAN to check out her abdomen. An image appeared of her bursting appendix, and the hospital sent us to the pediatric floor to prepare for surgery. Just after the sun rose, her gurney traveled to the Operating Room.

"Mommy, am I going to die?" She grabbed my hand as we moved down the sterile halls. The fluorescent lights buzzed and flickered. I heard her trembling voice and saw a singular tear slide down her cheek.

"Oh no, honey, I will see you in a few minutes. They are going to help you fall asleep, and when it is over, they will wake you up. We will be right here."

Tears rolled from her eyes to her ears. The anesthesiologist came in to talk to Alex. "And then, we will put a big tube down your throat to help you breathe during the surgery."

I glanced at Michael. *Why would he say that to an eight-year-old?* I tried to send Michael my question and concern telepathically, but he didn't see the message behind my eyes.

I leaned over to Alex and said, "You are stronger than you think. This will be over in no time, and when it is, you will feel better. Mom and Dad will be right here waiting when you wake up."

With that, she was gone. The three of us headed to the cafeteria to grab some breakfast while we waited.

Poor Robbie had gotten no sleep the night before, and you could see the dark discoloration under his eyes. I knew he was going to be grumpy for the next two days.

The surgery was a success, and within hours we were discharged.

That afternoon, the four of us climbed into our own beds and napped, not discussing the fact that we weren't heading up to New Hampshire even though we all already knew.

"Maybe we can go for the weekend," I said to Michael as we snuggled under the covers.

He nodded at me in agreement. "I think we should try. This family has been through too much."

He was right. I used to think we planned and executed our life perfectly. Now I felt lucky if I cooked toast without burning the bread. Too many times, my brain failed me, and this vacation was not going to be another failure added to my list.

My expectations for life had dropped significantly since November, and I would be damned if my kids didn't get a little escape from our life for a few days.

Chapter 18

Our mini-vacation to New Hampshire was supposed to be relaxing and fun, but instead, an air of melancholy draped over us. The trip became one night because Alexandria was afraid to walk upright due to the discomfort in her abdomen. It took about four days for her to tolerate walking, and any movement triggered a wail. Had she not been able to see the incision on her belly button, she would have been fine.

The last night of our scheduled vacation, we convinced Alex that she was well enough to travel.

The trip to the hospital mentally and physically drained Michael and I, but we kept the kids in the forefront of our mind. Packing up the car and traveling in the snow to the mountains seemed too overwhelming to tackle, but we wanted to get at least one night in. If we canceled the entire trip, the money would have gone down the toilet, and we couldn't afford to throw it away. On the last day, we piled into the car and headed to the White Mountains.

The house was perfect. It had two bedrooms, a kitchenette, a living room, and a tiny bathroom. It overlooked the snow-coated mountains that glistened in the sun. We brought hot chocolate from home and stopped at the corner store for some whipped cream.

The hot chocolate was the highlight of my twenty-four hours.

Robbie complained that there was no Wi-Fi, Alex complained that her belly hurt, and Michael and I struggled to make a fire in the wood-burning stove.

We ignored all the signs that this trip would be a disaster, and Michael and I tried to exude positivity to trick the kids into changing their attitudes. It was one of those moments where our intentions were sincere, but the universe had been telling us it wasn't a great idea.

The amount of packing for one night made us never want to come back again. We brought sheets and pillows and food for a twenty-four-hour trip, stuffing the car so full, Michael could barely see out the back window.

Once our trunk was packed like a sardine can and we pulled up to the house, we trekked through the crunchy, crystal white snow carrying bag after bag from the car to the house. Tomorrow we'd pack it all up and do it again.

"Mom? Where are we going to sleep?" Robbie asked, dropping his backpack on the hard wood floor. I looked around the cabin and saw a double bed, a couch, and a chair.

"I thought it was two bedrooms," I said to myself.

Michael glanced at me, as he dropped a bag of food on the small table.

"I must have read the listing wrong." I bit my bottom lip, adding vacation to my list of failures. "Oh, the couch must be a sleeper," I responded, not sure if that was true.

Robbie pulled the couch cushions off the couch and found a solid sofa. "Nope," he said, tossing the cushions on the floor.

Responsibility for not knowing the details of our stay triggered my heartbeat to increase. *I knew there were enough sleeping options for all of us, so why didn't I double check?* I questioned my brain and all the decisions I had screwed up over the past year. Even after surgery, my brain was still failing me.

"We'll make it work," I said, searching for a cot in the closet.

The empty closet stared back at me. We were out of options. One bed, one couch, one chair, and four people. I refused to give up. This night was supposed to be a break from our lives.

I pulled Michael into the kitchen and asked, "What do we do?"

Chapter 18

He weighed our options. "We could leave, or we could suck it up and make the best of it."

We decided to stay, but we needed to get creative to make it work.

"Robbie, you get the couch. Alex, you get the bed with me. Michael, you get the floor," I commanded.

Michael looked at me incredulously. "I can't sleep on the floor. I have to drive tomorrow and pack up the car. If you want me to be kind and happy tomorrow, I am not sleeping on the floor."

"But I can't sleep on the floor. I'm still recovering," I debated. "And so is Alex."

Michael placed his hands on my shoulders and gave me a little squeeze. He wrapped his arms around the back of my neck. "I know you want this," he whispered, "but this isn't what we imagined. I know it sounds crazy, but I think we should go home. We tried to make it work, but it isn't the right time."

I dropped my eyes.

"Maybe next year we can go on a trip when everyone is healthy. Don't let the cost of losing money influence your decision to stay if it is going to make all of us miserable."

Tears climbed while Michael and I stood in the corner of the dark, dingy cabin.

I wanted so badly to give the kids something positive that I forced this trip on everyone. Alex was recovering, I was technically still recovering, and Robbie just got dragged along for the ride.

Michael did his best to be helpful, but I knew the amount of packing, lifting, and carrying that I couldn't do fell onto him. I knew it wasn't fair to Michael or the kids to make them stay, and I knew that we were a family who needed to make decisions together.

"Does everyone want to go home?" I asked.

Robbie didn't answer, but his response hung within his body language. He shuffled toward me, carrying his backpack, and proceeded to put his shoes on.

"Can we go home?" Alex asked. She picked up her pillow and brought it to the door of the cabin.

"I am so sorry," I whispered to Michael. "This was a complete disaster. I don't know why I pushed for us to come here." Feeling defeated, all I wanted to do was allow my family an opportunity to relax and enjoy life for a moment, but the timing was all wrong.

Michael kissed me. "I give you an A for effort." He smiled at me and picked up our luggage. I felt foolish for thinking this trip would be a good idea.

It reminded me of when the kids were little, and I made them go to Thanksgiving, even though I knew it would be a disaster. When Robbie was a toddler and Alex was an infant, we went to Hank and Janet's house for dinner. Robbie was a runner, and he would run throughout the house without a second glance at all the uneven surfaces or sharp corners.

Robbie had just started talking and struggled with being understood by others. He would slam his head into the floor in frustration, and when these tantrums happened, I immediately had to place something soft under him so he wouldn't give himself a concussion.

Alex was a few months old at the time and was on a rigorous schedule. I was home with both kids on maternity leave and could barely juggle both of their needs. When one child tipped the routine, all the balls fell, and I struggled to get them up again.

That day, Michael was home with me, which naturally threw off the routine. Michael wanted to go to Janet and Hank's for Thanksgiving because they were the grandparents, and we hadn't been able to show off Alex's beautiful blue eyes or curly, black hair to the family yet. He didn't understand that Alex went down for a nap at ten a.m. on the dot or that Robbie would only eat dinosaur-shaped chicken nuggets cooked in the oven for lunch. He didn't realize that after Blue's Clues, Robbie went down for a nap, but only after Blue's Clues and no other show.

Our routine flew out the window between the disruption of our day with Michael being home and cooking for Thanksgiving. Getting to Janet and Hank's house meant that the afternoon nap would be late, and I prayed they would nap in the car.

I was a mess. Overwhelmed by the number of things that needed to get

Chapter 18

done, the change in the routine, and not knowing if Janet and Hank's house would be baby proofed enough to the point where I would feel safe with Robbie running around like a maniac, I cried. I didn't want to go.

"I don't think it's a good idea," I said to Michael. "Alex is teething, and I don't know if I trust the dog with Robbie. He hasn't been around animals before. I don't know if we will be able to watch his every move. Especially with so much activity in the house." I nudged him to see my perspective, as I wiped my eyes.

"We'll bring the pack and play, and if we can't watch him the way we need to, we'll put him in there until we can," Michael responded. "Ashley, it's my parents. We can't say no to my parents."

I nodded. I knew he was right, and if my parents were alive and hosting a holiday, I would demand we go too.

"Fine, but can we have a code word if things get out of control?" I asked. "How about Disney World," I said it more as a statement instead of a question. "If I ask someone if they have ever been to Disney World, that means we need to go."

Even when things were out of my control, I always figured out a way to regain control.

"Sure, Ashley." Michael sighed.

It's not that I didn't like his family, because they were great. It's just that I was the one responsible for my children day in and day out, and to make my life easier, I needed to make sure their life was easy and predictable. The best way to do that was to have a routine that we could follow every day, without exception, and traveling to Rhode Island for a big family meal was not my idea of easy.

Michael packed the pack-n-play, the portable high chair, a bag of toys, snack and food items, diapers, extra clothes, and Robbie's stuffed animal and blankie. He tossed them them into the car and I rearranged the order so I could access what I needed during the drive.

Our car looked like we were moving across the country, and Michael struggled to see out the rear window. I let Michael take control of the day, and I agreed to go along for the ride.

We did what we thought was right. We allowed our family to meet and spend time with our kids. We created holiday memories that our kids would never remember. We demonstrated how flexible we were as parents by allowing Robbie to eat as much dessert as he wanted. We did our best to bend to the expectations of everyone else, even though we both knew that in a perfect world, we would be home following our daily routine without a hiccup.

The reality of that Thanksgiving was that Robbie screamed every time we placed him in the pack-n-play. He spent most of the day there because we had to help cook, set the table, and clean the kitchen. When Robbie screamed, so did Alex. When Robbie traversed freely, he dodged furniture and people and ended up with a gash on his forehead from tripping on the runner and falling superman style on the hard wood floors into the door jamb.

We forgot the pacifiers, which would have been okay on a typical day when stores were open, but we were stuck with the gas station options, which was none.

I spent the majority of the day upstairs nursing, burping, and rocking Alex. I was alone with my child in the dark, crying in frustration to no one in particular.

By the time dessert was placed on the table, I was frantically asking everyone if they had been to Disney World. Michael was equally frazzled but appeared conflicted. He didn't want to leave his family with a sink full of dishes to clean up.

I didn't care how he felt. We had to go. According to family expectations, I went with him because it was right, but our kids were melting down, which meant I was melting down. I needed to get out of there. As Michael came up with an excuse to head home, I silently collected all their toys and baby equipment and dropped them at the front door to be brought out to the car.

Michael and I didn't speak on the way home. As we listened to Robbie label every car and truck he saw on the highway and Alex coo in her car seat, we both thought about the day we had just experienced and how things went so terribly off course. I felt like a crazy woman and didn't like it.

From that point forward, I decided that I wouldn't subject my family to

Chapter 18

experiences strictly to meet unrealistic expectations.

Now, here we were, packing up our car in New Hampshire after four hours of hell. It was more like four months of hell. I had fallen into the trap again, of forcing my family into making memories that they weren't emotionally or mentally ready to experience.

I was so desperate to get back to everyday life that I tried to force something as ordinary as a family vacation and it had backfired.

That Monday, the kids went back to school. For them, school was the symbol of normalcy.

Chapter 19

The following month I looked normal, and my old self seemed to be emerging from the cracks. Although faint, my sense of smell had returned, and the puffiness around my eyes decreased. I could walk around the house in the evening without sunglasses over my eyes, and read Alex hours of stories without taking a break.

That month, still technically recovering but feeling fine, I was the mother I never knew I always wanted to be. The kids and Michael were out of the house until three, and I could catch up on my talk shows while folding laundry. I lived in yoga pants and t-shirts, and it felt good not to have a plan or meet a deadline. The constant pressure to make the perfect pitch at work disappeared. Present in my skin, my home, and my life, I was living an alternate reality.

I tried to cook dinner twice a week for the family, which I had never done before. Even when I was home for those six weeks of maternity leave with Alex, I was a walking zombie who only consumed coffee and leftover chicken nuggets from Robbie's highchair. Those six weeks were miserable, and if that was my dress rehearsal of being a stay-at-home mom, it was a show I didn't want to experience. I hurried back to work as quickly as possible and told my husband that I was working an unfathomable number of hours for them and their happiness.

Michael and I had struggled in the early years because we were poor as

Chapter 19

church mice. The money from my parent's death awarded me enough money to pay for my college tuition. By the time I graduated, the money was gone.

When I became pregnant with Robbie, I worked at an advertising agency, with the sole responsibility of photocopying, setting up chairs and tables for meetings, and prepping packets of information for the guest executives. I was treated like an intern but somehow convinced them I was worth a measly paycheck. I wanted to be one of the industry's important people, so I killed myself working sixty hours a week, trying to prove myself.

When people approached me to compliment my outfit, or my shoes, or comment on the design of the presentation that they had no part in making, I glowed inside. I felt pride build inside me, and knew I was just as good at the job as they were.

But I needed someone to give me a chance.

When we first married, Michael always tinkered with his hobbies, and I found that most of our money went to trying out new projects. He dabbled in woodworking, painting, beer brewing, smoking meat, and carpentry. To support his hobbies, he worked at a local restaurant on the side, cooking in the kitchen. It was decent money and allowed him to sleep all day and stay up all night, but we never saw each other. We were two completely different people sharing one space and saw each other for dinner a few times a week. Michael was chained to work on the weekends, and I was chained to work during the work week.

When we had gotten married, the life we were living was not the picture-perfect life I had envisioned. At first, the idea of having no money and slowly working our way to success was a romantic idea that I held onto, even though it felt impossible. I knew it could happen because I saw it in almost every movie or read in every book.

Life was about overcoming difficulties, and for us, our dilemma was financial. We believed happiness would come when financial worry left. We thought happiness and success were determined by the number of people who looked at us and thought, "I want to be like them when I get married."

Michael and I never fought, but we also never saw each other. The only time we spent together was in the early mornings before I left for work.

I would lean over in our lumpy bed and kiss him. That was the first and only kiss of the day because I was fast asleep every night when he got home. Occasionally, that morning kiss would lead to other things, which would cause me to frantically rush through the house to get to work only a few minutes late instead of the fifteen it would take for me to move about at my average speed.

As the years progressed, I thought about our life and how our connection severed so quickly. I loved him. I did. But the stress of being broke was starting to get to me. I was tired of eating Rice-A-Roni every night and then going to work with my Kate Spade handbag. I mastered my second identity, pretending I lived a life I didn't.

We continued to live this charade. I talked to my girlfriends about keeping our marriage spicy, made plans to spend time with him, and even partook in his hobbies to create a greater personal connection. I thought that if we became more emotionally attached, general happiness would follow.

I had everything planned out. Two nights on the coast of Rhode Island, a romantic walk along the ocean, and dinner in the town. I imagined bubble baths, champagne, lingerie, and waking up mid-morning with chocolate-dipped strawberries.

I had convinced Michael to take off work for a long weekend to celebrate our second anniversary. I never told him, but our Discover card paid the entire weekend. He didn't ask, and he never paid attention to our spending. I opted to pay by credit card because I couldn't imagine telling my friends that I had spent my anniversary alone because we were broke.

My husband was working his barely above minimum wage job, and I needed something unique to experience with him. I needed something amazing to share with my friends. I wanted them to be jealous of the weekend we shared because I wanted them to look at our marriage as their goal.

Now, I saw how foolish I was. I worried about other people's perceptions of us and completely ignored the crumbling pillars holding my life together.

Nine months later, Robbie came barreling out of me, screaming at the top of his lungs. Michael and I left the hospital unprepared, even though we had nine months to figure it out. We collected the primary baby gear from

Chapter 19

our generous family and friends, but were mostly on our own with the little things, like food, clothes, and diapers.

I stayed home with Robbie for six weeks, but I couldn't get out of there quick enough. I had somehow procured a job as an advertising editor and was making my first actual salary. We no longer had to eat Ramen Noodles but could instead upgrade to chicken or beef any time we wanted.

Michael quit his job at the restaurant because I needed him home more than eighteen hours a week. When the nights got dark and chilly, and I fumbled with baby bottles and wipes, I needed him to share the responsibility. If I had to give up my job for a short time, so did he. Discover and Visa became our best friends, keeping us afloat throughout the shell-shock of life with a child.

After six weeks, I needed to get back to work. I happily welcomed deadlines and meetings that brought structure to my life. I couldn't seem to make decisions about diaper rash, allergies, or personal finances, but I could set up a fantastic conference room. Whenever someone complimented me, I reminded myself that some aspect of my life was going well.

Since I made the majority of the money, Michael needed to stay home with the baby. We could pay some childcare costs, but not a whole week, month, or year.

Michael's buddy from college, Greg, had started a General Contracting company, and with a bit of seed planting from me, Michael elicited enough courage to call and ask for a job. He had no real experience, but he at least knew how to work the tools. That started our new routine. I worked Monday through Friday, Michael worked Thursday, Friday, and Saturday, Robbie went to daycare two days a week, and Sunday was family day. It wasn't easy, but it worked.

Fast forward two years, and we found ourselves in the same predicament. The only difference was, this time, we had to talk about moving to accommodate another human. Our one-bedroom apartment was barely large enough for Michael and me, but we crammed Robbie and all the baby gear in there. Now, to have another baby was something I couldn't fathom.

"We need to move," I said to Michael, with my four-month swollen belly threatening to unsnap my jeans. "We have to," I repeated.

That night we sat down, Robbie in his crib sleeping, with a yellow legal pad in front of us, breaking down the bills and our income, as we had done many times before. We knew that living in a tiny one-bedroom apartment with two small kids was borderline child neglect, and neither one of us wanted that for our kids. Our kids deserved sidewalks and established trees and their own bedroom.

The problem was that I needed to work, and I was not willing to leave my job. I had been there too long and had established connections that would lead me up the corporate ladder. I wasn't ready to sacrifice all I had built or start again at the bottom.

Michael's work was seasonal, and the pay was inconsistent. Greg had been more than accommodating when hiring and training Michael, but our life needed more stability.

We found a two-bedroom in an old Victorian house in an elegant, established neighborhood thirty miles west of Boston. We couldn't afford it, but we loved it. We signed on the dotted line and relied on our credit card when things got tough.

We unlocked the apartment door two months after Alexandria made her appearance. I stood in the kitchen, with a baby on my hip and Robbie toddling at my feet. That weekend, Jason, Tiffany, and Amanda came over to help us unload the U-Haul and set up the apartment.

That entire year was a whirlwind, and honestly, I think I slept or cried through most of it. I went back to work six weeks after Alex was born, and the new commute into Boston practically killed me. My commute tripled in time, and most days, I was mentally and emotionally distressed when I walked through the front door.

Michael, jobless once I returned to work, stayed home with both kids, and we saved on daycare costs but paid more in commuting costs and time away from home. It was not the situation I imagined, but I was in the throes of motherhood and employment, and I couldn't change it.

As we established ourselves in the community, we made friends with other parents. Michael relied heavily on the town library and immersed

Chapter 19

himself and both kids into the Mommy and Me support group. Suddenly, people invited us to barbeques and picnics, and play dates. This connection presented Michael with an opportunity that created the emotional stability we had been craving for years.

Lina, one of the moms in the playgroup, was a teacher in a neighboring town. She knew a little about Michael and how he was a tinkerer and had worked for a general contractor. She told him that working for a school was a great job if you were a parent because it provided family-friendly hours, retirement, and a consistent paycheck. Michael and I had fought many times over stability and although working in a school wasn't something we ever considered, it made sense.

Except for one thing. "But I'm not a teacher, and I don't have any sort of teaching degree," he said to Lina.

"You don't need a teaching degree to be a custodian," Lina said. "All you need is not have a criminal record."

Michael shrugged but brought it up that night over dinner. I didn't love the idea of having a custodian for a husband. Still, I was mentally and emotionally exhausted and knew that if he had a steady paycheck coming in, I wouldn't have to kill myself quite so often to create incredible output at work.

It was a long process, but when Alex was six months old, we started another transition. Michael went to work Monday through Friday, kids went to daycare full time, and I commuted into the city every day. We suddenly had a regular schedule like every other family in America.

We had an opportunity to pay off debt and start living life the way I pictured it.

Now, I looked around my kitchen, with the granite counter tops and stainless-steel appliances, and wondered how we got here. The road was hard and bumpy, and I dedicated my life to work, to prove to all the doubters that, yes, I was successful. I had a beautiful house, a brand-new car, and clean kids to show for it.

A reminder of the emptiness I had experienced in the past opened up within me, and I questioned if the road to get here was worth the sacrifice.

With surprise, I realized I hadn't been to work in four months and I never felt quite so satisfied.

Chapter 20

It had been nine weeks since my surgery, and I was scheduled for a week of appointments in Boston, all on different days. An MRI, the endocrinology team, ophthalmology team, and my neurosurgeon highlighted my calendar.

I felt better, so I convinced myself everything was good.

Michael couldn't take off work for the entire week, so I asked my family and friends to take me into the city.

Jessica brought me on Monday to meet with Dr. Walker. We sat in the cramped waiting room. The receptionist at the desk told me that Dr. Walker was still in surgery and would be with us shortly. We entertained ourselves with the vast array of magazines on the coffee table in front of us.

The newspaper caught my eye, and I pulled the front page close. In big bold letters, I read the word I'd been hearing about for months. Coronavirus. That crazy virus in Asia and Europe had made its presence known on the Western coast of America and had moved its way to New England.

I hadn't paid attention to the developing news story because my health problems consumed me, but the virus was here in Massachusetts. Articles about the transmission, cases, and testing shortages filled the page. I glanced around the room, wondering about the people next to me.

The receptionist at the front desk called my name while I read about Italy. Italian doctors had to choose which patients they could treat at the hospital and which patients they would send home to die.

I put the paper down, and Jessica and I followed the nurse into Dr. Walker's office.

Dr. Walker fluttered about wearing blue scrubs and pearl earrings. I wondered if she removed her earrings for surgery or put them under a scrub cap to keep her ears clean. She pulled up my account on her computer to show me the MRI results from the day before.

"Hi Ashley," she said.

I introduced her to Jessica, and they shook hands.

"The surgery was a success. We removed two-thirds of the tumor, and your optic nerve is now getting blood and oxygen. That was the purpose of the surgery. To alleviate the pressure on your eyes and improve your sight."

I nodded in understanding, although I didn't like to hear "improve your sight" instead of "correct your sight."

"Take a look here," she said, pointing to the computer. "That right there is what is left. We got out as much as we could. It was a tough tumor. Probably one of the toughest we've had in the past six months. You currently have two millimeters of space between the edge of the remaining tumor and your optic nerve. You have two choices." She paused before continuing. "A third surgery or radiation. You will have radiation no matter what because the tumor has encased your carotid artery. We can go in again and try to remove more, or we can skip the surgery and go straight to radiation."

Wait, what? I thought the surgery was a success. Why would a third surgery be on the table? My mind buzzed with chatter, and I couldn't entirely focus.

She waited for a response, busying herself with a pile of paper on her desk.

"I am not having another surgery," I said with my arms crossed.

Dr. Walker nodded. "Okay. I agree. I didn't want to go back in either. I think we got all we could, but I would go in again if you wanted me to try."

I thought back to my recovery. The blood, the vomiting, nausea, the loss of smell, the choking, the brain fog. I would not have them go in again. I couldn't scare my daughter again for the slight chance of removing more. I refused to go through that entire recovery process for a third time, just to have radiation down the road.

Chapter 20

Jessica didn't say a word until we were safely in our car, sitting in the quiet parking garage. She turned to me. "Are you okay?"

I nodded. "I just don't understand. I thought I was in the clear. Why did no one tell me? I had an MRI a few days after my last surgery. Why did no one prepare me?"

I thought about work and how they expected me back in three weeks. I dreaded the conversation with HR, explaining that I needed more treatment and didn't know when or if I could return.

I hated feeling out of control, with my life in the hands of others. All I could do was trust that they knew what they were doing.

I told Michael about my options that night after the kids went to bed. "What do you think?" I asked him.

"I think you have to do the radiation. If she said that radiation would be the last step, I think you have to do it now. It's been a tough year on the family, and I think we need to just power through. Eventually, you'll go back to work," he rationalized.

The following day, after the kids got on the bus, Michael and I climbed into the car to head into Boston for my next appointment that week. This time, we saw Dr. Chalksky, the Neuro-Ophthalmologist, who checked my eyes. He had a fellow doctor with him and explained every step of the evaluation. I appreciated his explanations because they gave me insight into why my eyes weren't working.

"See this?" he said, pointing to the computer screen. He wasn't speaking to me, but I followed along, staring at his computer.

His fellow nodded.

"The surgeon had to stop. See, right here," he pointed at the carotid artery, which looked like a donut on the screen. The black middle was the artery, and the white ring was the tumor. "Had she continued in this area, she would have died. And see this?" he said, pointing to the remaining gray blob. "She needs radiation. If she doesn't, it will grow, she will go blind, and she will die."

I threw a glance at Michael because this was the second time Dr. Chalksky had made that prediction. I was not quite sure if I was reassured by his honesty or terrified by the possible outcome.

Later in the day, Michael said, "You have to get the radiation."

I nodded.

The next day, I met with Neuro-Endocrinology. Tiffany took me into the city and sat with me while they drew blood and ran hormone tests. We had a two-hour gap between the lab work and the appointment, so we grabbed a bite to eat at a small sandwich shop.

"What were all those vials for?" she asked me as I drank my Coke and ate my chips.

"What was it not for?" I responded. "They were checking my thyroid and adrenal. The pituitary gland controls every other gland in the body, so when the pituitary gland is out of whack, so are all the others. My tumor was large, which means that it can cause hormone deficiencies. They checked my prolactin, estrogen, LH, and FSH. Those are all female reproductive hormones. Also, my cortisol, which controls my energy, and my thyroid. So far, my cortisol and thyroid have been low, so I am taking medication."

"Huh. If they know you are low, why are they still testing you?" she asked.

"Because the hormones malfunction over time. My estrogen last time was undetectable. The first question every doctor asks is, "Do you want to have any more kids?" and when I say no, they ignore the fact that I am not producing any estrogen. I think there is medication to pump it up, but if I don't want kids, they'll let it be. That's why I have night sweats, hot flashes, and hair loss. I haven't had a period since I went off the pill in November. It could be menopause…or at least that is what they said. I think they are hoping my estrogen level will naturally increase."

I felt weird talking with Tiffany about how I didn't want any more children. I knew she wanted kids, but she never found the right person. She wanted her family to happen naturally, so she never investigated IVF or adoption.

"I recently went on thyroid meds because my thyroid level had slowly been decreasing and is now in the borderline range," I said.

Tiffany nodded, the terminology over her head.

I checked my watch. "You know what? We should head back. My appointment is in twenty minutes."

Chapter 20

We sat in front of Dr. Vari, the Neuro-Endocrinologist, who again pulled up my most recent MRI. "Well," she said, "It looks like your tumor has fallen down a bit, which is great. Tell me, how are you feeling?" she asked.

I knew that hormone changes contributed to most of my weird symptoms, so I told her about all the odd things I had been experiencing.

"Well, I still get night sweats, I still get lightheaded, and I still haven't lost any weight. My memory is a mess. The other day, I was baking cookies for the kids and left them in the oven to cool. The next day, I went to cook dinner, and the smoke alarm was going off because the cookies were still sitting there! Another day, I cooked pizza for Robbie, and I cut him a slice and kept the rest of the pizza in the oven to stay warm. I looked at Robbie's empty plate and couldn't believe he ate that whole pizza! Except he didn't. The pizza sat in the oven for two days before I saw it. I swear I am going to burn down the house. I can't multitask anymore, I can't make sense of our finances, and I get overwhelmed very easily with life."

"That brain fog could be a result of your low thyroid. You were never actually below average but were steadily falling, so we put you on a preventative level of medication. It could also be because of your estrogen. Women going through menopause often complain of a fogginess that interferes with their functioning. It could also be because of the sheer size of your tumor. They got a lot out, but there is still a lot there. The tumor could be pushing against some tissue that is interfering with your memory," Dr. Vari explained. "How is your sleep?"

"Perfect, although I need a few hours less sleep now than I ever did before."

"And if you don't mind me asking, how is your sex life? Do you still have vaginal dryness?"

I looked at Tiffany and blushed. She and I were close, but we weren't so close that we exchanged sex tips and techniques. Plus, it was her brother I was talking about, which made it more uncomfortable, but this was my health and life, so I pressed on.

"Honestly, amazing. There is no vaginal dryness, and my sex life has never been better. Seriously, I feel like a completely different person. I feel like a teenager." It was true. Instead of hiding from my parents, I was hiding from my children.

"Have you had your period yet?" She asked.

I shook my head no.

"Just be careful. You can still get pregnant."

I nodded in understanding. "Okay."

"Now, for your results. Your cortisol is still low, and you are looking a tad bit puffy. We need to decrease your prednisone just a bit. Your estrogen is detectable but still low. I am still holding out hope that it will rebound, especially since your sex life has improved. Your thyroid is officially below average, so we are going to bump up your daily dosage. We will repeat the tests in six months and modify them from there. I am also putting you on a B Complex vitamin to help with your memory. Any questions?"

I shook my head no, and Tiffany and I headed home. *One more appointment, and then the week is over.* My next appointment was over the phone, saving me a trip into Boston.

The following day, I packed the kids their lunches and threw in some extra homemade cookies and chocolate-covered pretzels. I grabbed two napkins and wrote, "You are berry special. Have a lovely day!" and taped it to the Juicy Juice boxes before zipping up the lunch boxes and placing them in their backpacks. "Kids! Breakfast!" I hollered up the stairs.

The kids bounded down the stairs to find two glasses of orange juice and two plates full of waffles and bacon at their seats.

"Thanks, Mom." Robbie poured syrup over his homemade waffles.

"Can I have some more juice?" Alex asked, downing her glass.

I happily traipsed around the kitchen, proud of the breakfast I cooked.

Michael came around the corner, and I grabbed the back of his neck, and gave him a deep, intense kiss. I looked into his eyes and said, "Good morning."

He grinned at me, not quite sure what to make of my sudden display of affection. The kids were in the dining room, out of our view, so Michael grabbed my waist and pulled me closer to him, and kissed me gently on the nose.

"I'm going to do it, Michael. Today I will find out about radiation, and I will do it with a smile on my face. Do you know why? Because I realized

Chapter 20

that you and the kids are the most important thing in my life. You deserve to have me present and in the moment. And I am going to do it, and I am going to get better, and I am going to be better for you and the kids. Do you know why? Because we deserve to be happy." I squeezed him and turned around to pour him a hot mug of coffee.

He took it graciously and sat at the table with the kids. I had convinced him to take one more day off this week to sit with me for the Radiology Oncologist appointment. This appointment was going to determine the final chapter of my journey.

"Ten minutes, you guys. Finish getting ready and get outside for the bus." The kids brushed their teeth, and headed out into the cold air.

"So, I heard at work," Michael said to me, "that this virus thing is kind of crazy. I heard that the governor might start shutting things down." California and New York already shut down in the hope of containing the virus and prevent further outbreaks. Massachusetts had not yet been hit hard, but a big cluster from a business conference a few weeks ago flooded the news.

"I hope it doesn't come to that," I said. *Seriously, I have radiation to get through.* I didn't want to worry about catching a virus while getting my treatments. I didn't know what radiation treatment would entail, but I automatically thought of cancer, fatigue, and sickness.

My appointment with Dr. Landry, the Radiology Oncologist, was short and nondescript. I signed into Zoom and waited for him to join us.

An older man with gray hair and a beard filled my computer screen. He told me my tumor was no big deal and that he was confident it would never grow back. If he wasn't worried, then neither was I. The idea of being done with this part of my life encouraged me to continue to think positively.

"You will come into the hospital for twenty-five days, Monday through Friday," he explained.

Wait, what? Twenty-five days? I thought radiation was quick and easy. In and out. One zap, and then I was done. "Wow. I didn't realize it would be that lengthy," I said.

"Well, because we are so close to the brain and important structures, such as your optic nerve, we need to increase the frequency and decrease the level of radiation you receive each day. You will get twenty-five twenty-minute treatments to zap the tumor and kill the cells slowly. If the number of treatment days was shorter, you would be at increased risk for eye damage," he explained.

"Okay. I understand," I said, my spirits dropping.

He explained that the only symptom I would feel was fatigue, and I would be back to work within a week of my final treatment.

"When do we start?" I asked anxiously.

"We are going to start April thirteenth, and you will come in until May eighteenth. You'll get a schedule every Friday, but you must stay flexible," he continued.

I didn't have any other questions to speak of, so I flipped off my computer and looked at Michael. "April thirteenth. That's soon. What are we going to do?" I asked him.

It was exactly one month away, which gave me enough time to figure out childcare.

Michael pulled me in close and whispered, "We have a month to figure it out, but for now, I have you. Alone. In this house. With no kids. And great news. You are on the final leg." He slowly kissed my earlobes and I breathed in his cologne.

"You smell amazing." I hugged his body and allowed my stress and anxiety to melt away at his touch.

He led me upstairs to our bedroom, where all my inhibitions disappeared. I didn't worry about the kids or my health. I felt loved and desired, and allowed him to sculpt my body, rubbing his hand up and down my legs, arms, breasts, and torso. He leaned into me, and the only thing I felt was complete lust and desire. I had no idea how we had gotten here, but I was enjoying every moment.

With no one around, I allowed myself to disappear into him, and when I emerged, I became a confident, curvy, assertive woman. It was who I always knew I was but was afraid to be. I held onto these moments because I knew that life could be complicated and connections could be lost.

I wanted to be who we were that first night together when we learned about the intricacies that made us who we were. I always wanted to discover who he was and who he was becoming, and grow beside him like the random couples we admired enjoying their time together at the sandwich or coffee shop. I needed to grow with him instead of away from him. These thoughts ran through my mind as I lay next to him, naked, tracing the lines of his body with my fingers.

"I am so in love with you," I said, turning my face toward his.

He took his hand into mine and said, "Ditto." He kissed my fingers and nuzzled against me.

Life felt right for the first time in a long time, and I snuggled into Michael's bare body and thought of all the positives Timmy had brought us.

Part Three

I'm thankful for it all. The lows and the lessons, and the highs and the blessings. For every setback, there is a comeback, and I am thankful for the ride.
—E.D. Hackett

Chapter 21

"Hello, this is Mr. Snyder at Woodhaven Elementary School," my voicemail said. "Due to the coronavirus pandemic, the governor has issued an order that all schools will close their brick and mortar instruction. As of Monday, March sixteenth, all schools will be closed for two weeks. Please stay tuned for further information regarding your child's education."

I replayed the message, unsure how this had become our reality, and texted Michael, but he didn't get back to me until his drive home that afternoon. By then, the kids had barreled through the door, squealing about the craziness of their day. I had spent the day watching CNN, hoping to catch up on what I had missed over the past month.

I listened to the newscaster explain how the Boston area saw a recent uptick in cases. It sounded like the spread was exponential because people could spread the virus while asymptomatic. Health officials thought that people could spread the disease without showing symptoms and that cases were likely to spread among activities involving large groups, such as weddings and cruise ships. And school.

Visions of packed school buses and poorly ventilated classrooms filled my mind.

I texted Jessica, but she didn't respond. I imagined her running around her classroom, keeping the kids quiet while stuffing two weeks of work into their backpacks.

Robbie and Alex sat at the kitchen table, eating a slice of homemade pizza I had made an hour before to keep myself busy.

"Mom, we don't have school for two weeks," Robbie said.

I nodded, checking the time to see when Michael would arrive.

"Mom, I have some papers from my teacher in my backpack. She said it was important," Alex said between bites.

I looked at her backpack, stuffed with her lunch box, workbooks, artwork, and desk supplies. I made a mental note to look at it over the weekend when Michael was with me, double-checking all the information.

"Well, what did your teacher say?" I asked them both, waiting to see what they knew before telling them something different.

"Nothing. Just that there was a contagious virus, and we have to stay home to stay safe," Alex said.

"We will be back in two weeks," Robbie added.

"Well, actually, the Governor was on television today, and he told us that we had to stay home from work and school. Everything is closed except for grocery stores, gas stations, and banks. Hopefully, it will only be two weeks, but it might be longer," I explained.

I didn't know how this would affect us with radiation and now possibly no income for Michael.

Both kids nodded. They behaved like it was customary not to go to school in the middle of March. I silently thanked God that I was home during this time to care for them during the school closure. Childcare would be one less complication that dominated my mind.

That night, Michael and I pulled out all the documents from the school. The general consensus was that they didn't know what was happening. The tentative plan was a two-week time out because the novel coronavirus had a two-week incubation period.

As scheduled, Michael would go to work to clean all the classrooms from top to bottom. I asked God to keep him safe and healthy, and thanked Him for a consistent paycheck.

The following two weeks were a time of utter chaos in our household.

Chapter 21

There was no bedtime, no alarm clock, and no need to get dressed. Robbie had gotten into video games a few years earlier, and Alex still occupied her free time playing with her toy animals and stuffies. Of course, being home for two weeks straight with no plans was tiring in and of itself. The kids ate many snacks all day long, and I found myself in the kitchen doing dishes on an hourly basis.

I started to notice a change in my urgency to keep the house clean and in order. I still had the housecleaner do the big tasks, like clean out the fridge, wash the baseboard, and wipe down the cabinets, but I slacked in the daily tasks that plagued us every day. Instead of folding laundry the moment the dryer dinged, I let it sit in an overflowing heap on the couch until I got around to it. Instead of wiping down the bathroom sinks to keep them sparkly clean, I let the toothpaste build up until the basin was streaked white, and toothpaste residue distorted the mirror.

Keeping the house clean wasn't a priority right now. In the age of the coronavirus, it wasn't like anyone was coming over.

Then the housecleaner stopped coming because she was an unessential employee. It was too risky to have a stranger in the house, and all the housework fell back to me.

I had radiation coming up in two weeks, and I was afraid that she would bring the invisible germs from her other houses to mine. I didn't know where she had been or who had sneezed or coughed on her recently, so I thanked her for her time and accepted a filthy house in our future.

After she stopped coming, we had no reason to keep the house clean and in order. I was lucky if the carpets got vacuumed once every two weeks, but I didn't care, and I found that it didn't bother me the way it did before my diagnosis. Without working, I discovered my identity was in jeopardy, and keeping a house that would impress the neighbors was no longer a priority.

Two days before the kids were scheduled to go back to school, the Governor extended the stay-at-home order for another two weeks. Suddenly, the kids were no longer on vacation. They completed their schoolwork on the computer, and I fought with technology, unable to sign into one of their many academic platforms. I forgot the countless passwords to an overwhelming amount of apps.

It was a trying time for me because of the added responsibility. Besides catching up on my shows and straightening up the house, I was now in charge of my children's education. I could no longer lounge around in my bathrobe because the kids were on Zoom calls with their teachers periodically throughout the day.

I became a scheduler and scheduled school time and chore time and fun time and family time.

"If I wanted to be a teacher, I would have been a teacher," I complained to Jason one night on the phone while sipping on a glass of wine. "I have no idea what I am doing with the math. I just don't understand why you can't just add eight and three. Why the diagrams and seventy-five steps? Just add it. Use your fingers. I think I'm going to teach them how we learned math. We can do basic math, and how we learned it is just fine." I shuddered, realizing that I sounded like our grandmother when she tried to teach me how to knit or cook.

"Ash, it's okay. It's a global pandemic. The entire world has shut down. I really wouldn't worry about it."

"You know, a year ago, I would have told you that they needed to excel so that Robbie could get into the Gifted and Talented program and Alex would be in the highest reading level in her class. But the new me doesn't care." I paused, taking a sip of wine. "You know why? Because it isn't that important. As long as they are happy and well-rounded people, what more can I ask for?" I asked these questions to myself more than Jason, and he knew I didn't want or need a response.

He knew I was rationalizing my decision to let them take a break, even though my natural expectation would have been that they pushed themselves. I realized that I put undue pressure on them so that others would compliment them and me on their accomplishments. Now all I cared about was their mental well-being.

"Ashley, Ellie is in the same boat. School is a shit show right now. Melinda doesn't know how to teach, and most days, Ellie ends up crying and storming out of the room because she just doesn't get it. And Melinda doesn't get

Chapter 21

how Ellie doesn't get it. Seriously, give yourself a break. You guys have been through hell this year."

Our conversation shifted to my upcoming radiation and how going to the hospital during the pandemic was causing massive anxiety. I didn't want to do it, knowing that I might catch a deadly virus and pass it onto my family, but I didn't want to wait either.

This chapter had to end. I needed to move on with my life. I didn't want to tell anyone how afraid I was because if the doctor felt it was safe, I had to trust him. Plus, I didn't want to project my fear onto my kids.

They already noticed that we never left the house. We risked a trip to the grocery store once a month, and besides that, we never saw anyone. We were practically prisoners in our home. It was a good thing we liked each other.

"Let me know if there is anything I can do to help," Jason said.

I told him I would call him with any changes to the radiation plan.

To help pass the days, old Ashley kicked in and created an hour-by-hour schedule for each child. I jotted down their classroom obligations, outdoor time to fulfill Physical Education, art projects, music lessons, and what I liked to call Home Economics. It was never too early to teach the kids how to vacuum, dust, or help cook dinner.

My schedule chart was beautiful. It was color-coded for each person, and motivational stickers decorated the list to inspire them to succeed. I smiled proudly at my creation, and showed it to them with pride.

I realized three days later that for the schedule to work, I had to practically be a drill sergeant telling them what to do hour after hour. Tired of being the inflexible one, I pulled the plug, and we went back to chaos.

We had nowhere to go, so what was the urgency? If they wanted to help me clean or didn't, did it matter? No. If they didn't do it, did it make a difference? Again, no.

I started to focus on them as people instead of little worker bees. Sure, being responsible was important, but we were living in a global pandemic during a public and personal health emergency. I threw out all the expectations that had previously dictated how we lived.

Michael went with the flow because he wasn't home and wasn't making the kids' day-to-day decisions. He supported the daily schedule, assisted with family dinners, and participated in what I labeled "Family Fun Time," which often ended up being a movie or a game night.

I realized we could still have a good time without me micromanaging everyone's lives. When I relaxed, I even caught myself laughing at Robbie's jokes. I now found his jokes hilarious, when before my diagnosis, I barely cracked a smile. There had been a shift in my personality and mindset, and I had five months of staying home to thank for it.

Chapter 22

"Happy Anniversary!" Michael exclaimed as he carried out a small cake that read '13 and Counting'. He and the kids made a marble cake from scratch and the kids decorated it. Thirteen candles sat on the cake to celebrate every year of our marriage. Some were long and short to symbolize the highs and lows of love, and some were trick candles to represent all the trying times. Michael created that analogy himself, and I wondered when he became so sentimental.

It was the best cake I had ever tasted because the kids helped make it. I started to realize that everything was better when made from the heart.

The kids quickly ate their cake and then left the room to attend to their video games, and Michael and I reminisced about our wedding. It was one of the happiest days of my life because it was so simple. At the time, I didn't realize how beautiful simple could be, but now, looking back, I appreciated the modest, stripped-down love we showed during the event.

I thought about my grandmother and grandfather and how much they had sacrificed to take care of Jason and me. My grandfather had passed away before meeting Michael, which made me sad because my Grampy had a kind soul and loved everyone he met. I knew he would have loved Michael, and they would have bonded over their creative minds.

I remembered Grampy at his fortieth wedding anniversary party, wearing a button-down shirt and slacks with his sparkling white New Balance sneakers.

When he was a boy, he lived in an orphanage for most of his childhood and didn't have new clothes or shoes. Not having those necessities embarrassed him, and he often talked about the importance of clean shoes.

When he grew up and got a job at the local factory, he purchased his sneakers and kept them clean, wiping them down daily. He prided himself in always having clean shoes that fit, and New Balance sneakers were his favorite.

Michael, Jason, Gramma, and I changed into sneakers at the wedding reception in memory of him. Some of my favorite photos were of the four of us all dressed up with our feet in the air, showing off our new white sneakers.

"You look beautiful!" Gramma had exclaimed as she pulled my veil out over my shoulders to admire the delicate embroidery on the ends. I stood in front of the full-length mirror, twirling in my dress to see how difficult it might be to dance in.

"I hope the train doesn't fall when I'm dancing," I sashayed my hips and rolled my shoulders.

"I will be out there with you, doing a jig," she replied.

I couldn't imagine Gramma dancing in the middle of the floor with all the young folk busting a move.

"I can't wait to dance with you," I said.

I couldn't believe that I was getting married. I was twenty-five years old, but I had lived with Michael, to Gramma's dismay, since I was twenty-two. She had been appalled at first, but once we got engaged, her scowl lifted.

Michael and I had struggled those first few years and lived with various roommates in the city, trying to make ends meet. We were determined to take whatever money we received at the wedding to find an apartment of our own.

Gramma had placed her hands on my hips to interrupt the dance party going on in my head. "Ashley, I know you aren't much of a traditionalist, but I wanted to give you your mother's locket. I received her jewelry after the accident and couldn't seem to part with this one." She pulled out a heart-shaped locket that looked tarnished and worn and beautiful all at the same time. She separated the two sides, and inside I found a picture of Mom and

Chapter 22

Dad on one side and Jason and me on the other.

I wrapped my hand around the heart and felt tears build behind my eyes. "Oh, Gramma! This is beautiful."

"Now you have something borrowed or something old. Or it can be both borrowed and old." I tucked the necklace into my bra against my heart so that I could keep my parents close. I had wanted it to be our little secret and said a prayer to them, asking them to watch over my marriage.

I still couldn't believe I was getting married. I had always imagined that Michael would be my husband, but I never really believed that day would come. I had always thought I would have a big wedding with an expensive dress and flowers everywhere, but our lack of finances and the life insurance money gone meant that we had to embrace a modest wedding.

I had told Michael that we would renew our vows somewhere extravagant, like the Caribbean or Hawaii when we were rich. I was determined to make that day happen and have the wedding I had always dreamed about, but now, in 2020, I questioned my motives.

"Michael," I said, taking another bite of cake, "Would you still want to renew our vows in Hawaii like we always dreamed about?"

"No," he said.

A look of hurt and surprise crossed my face.

"I mean, yes, I would like to renew our vows, of course, but we don't need all that fanfare. All we need is our kids by our side and us. That's it."

I smiled and leaned toward him. "Yeah, I feel like life has kicked us to the ground, and although an expensive trip halfway around the world would be nice, it wouldn't be true to who we are."

"You mean who we have become?" he asked me.

I nodded. "This year has been eye-opening. It's shown me so much about life. We don't need all of this," I said, spreading my arms, palm up, like Vanna White. "What we need is this," I pointed to the photo album and the photos on the wall. "People we love. That's all we need."

Michael nodded and kissed me on the lips. "Happy Anniversary," he said as he poured two glasses of wine. "To us."

"To love. And to our family."

We clinked glasses and celebrated another year of life together.

***

The following day, I received a phone call from Dr. Landry's assistant, explaining that they postponed my radiation.

"What do you mean?" I asked incredulously. I had just coordinated childcare, and Michael had requested vacation, and I had finally felt like maybe all of my ducks were in a row. Until now.

"Well, cases have been steadily rising, and now our hospital admissions are rising. We cannot allow elective procedures due to the health risk and safety of others. Your treatment is urgent but not emergent. Your tumor is slow-growing, so we feel it is safest if we postpone it," the assistant said.

"But I just got childcare sorted." I sighed a deep huff. "How long exactly are we talking?" I asked.

"We have you tentatively scheduled for July fifteenth to August nineteenth. If things remain dire, we may reschedule again, but we hope to complete your treatment then."

I hung up the phone, feeling frustrated and defeated.

I just want to be done! Why is this happening to me?

Frustration led to anger, and I stormed upstairs to pull out the gratitude journal Michael had given me. It had sat on my dresser for weeks because my head was in the right place, but now I felt my optimism falling. Sure, I had to manage the anxiety the pandemic created and learn how to homeschool my children, but we figured out our routine reasonably quickly, and life felt good.

Now, life felt like a game of Whack-A-Mole. Every time life threw us an obstacle, I quickly slammed it down with my positive thinking. As soon as it disappeared, another problem popped up out of nowhere. I was so close to the end, yet I now had to wait another three months. That meant three more months of me not being able to return to work. The length of this entire process was starting to weigh me down, and I could feel myself sinking underwater, unable to breathe or kick my way up to get air.

***

As spring turned to summer, the cool morning breezes turned to hot,

Chapter 22

sticky, stagnant air. School had officially ended, and my subpar teaching somehow advanced the kids to the next grade. The state restrictions slowly lifted, but masks still needed to be worn outside the home.

The government's new vocabulary, like 'social distancing' and 'flatten the curve,' became household words. The coronavirus became the main news topic, and we couldn't seem to get away from this new normal. Massachusetts cases peaked in April, and we slowly descended the other side of the mountain.

Robbie and Alex didn't quite understand why we couldn't see friends or family. Since March, they had been out of the house a handful of times. One time, I took them to Target, with masks affixed, to create some sense of normalcy.

The lake we frequented closed for the summer, and we weren't comfortable going to a beach with random people who ignored the health precautions. Being around strangers and not knowing what they touched or where they came from caused increased anxiety and increased suspicion.

I already had enough going on in my life. I did not need to contract an unknown virus on top of it. I needed to get my radiation done, and I needed to get it done safely.

The kids adjusted to their new summer routine. They slept in late, went to bed late, ate whenever they were hungry, and occasionally helped me around the house. The house slowly fell apart at the seams, but I reminded myself we were living in a pandemic.

Michael worked nonstop over the summer, cleaning classrooms, disinfecting furniture, and making changes determined by the Department of Education. School in the fall was questionable, but the schools needed to prepare for all scenarios.

Michael wore a gown, goggles, gloves, and a mask when working, and stripped down to his boxers and bathrobe in the mudroom when he returned home from work. I made him immediately shower, just in case. My number one goal this summer was to stay healthy and keep the family safe.

I knew I was in a tricky spot when radiation came. No one was allowed in the hospital with me, and I couldn't subject Michael to the complaining and fighting that would ensue if we dragged Robbie and Alex to the hospital every day. We lived just far enough away from Boston that the time it would take to exit and re-enter the driveway would be four hours each day. Robbie and Alex would drive Michael crazy if they were locked in a car with him waiting for me to finish my treatments. They might be able to handle it once, but not twenty-five times.

As much as I wanted to protect my children, I knew I had to bend at some point. I had to accept that they would eventually be at risk, so I might as well put them at risk with someone I trusted. I called Jessica.

"Hey, Jess. How's your summer been?"

I missed seeing her and hearing her laugh. She and I continued to text a few times each week, but our weekend breakfast dates had come to a crashing halt, and Girl Scouts ceased back in March. Jessica had invited the kids over numerous times, but I couldn't risk it.

"Good. Somehow busy, despite everything."

"I have a favor to ask of you, and please say no if it is too much. I will completely understand." I explained that I needed a sitter for four hours every day from mid-July to the end of August. "We haven't seen anyone since March," I added.

She agreed, and we worked out a social contract. My kids would no longer go to Target, even when they drove me crazy because they were dying of boredom or had nothing to do. Jessica and Malia agreed to omit playdates until the end of my radiation.

I found that everyone handled this quarantine business differently, and it all depended on your comfort level with getting sick. It wasn't always about being asymptomatic and getting others sick, which was just as big of an issue. It seemed more about how comfortable you were getting sick for yourself and your immediate family.

Some people still refused to wear masks because they said it violated their rights to be an American. This illness was highly controversial and political, and you never knew which way people swung on the issue.

Although I was cramping their social life, I appreciated that she was willing to set things aside to keep me safe. Having a sitter for the next six weeks

Chapter 22

alleviated a lot of stress, and I could feel my body relax, knowing that I only had to worry about myself. Providing my kids with social opportunities was a bonus.

Mom-guilt slid away from me. I knew the kids were jealous of their friends who went to the ocean or swimming or camping, when I told them repeatedly we couldn't leave the house.

It was harder for Michael to get off work for the majority of the summer, especially during the pandemic, but he could work things out with the Superintendent at the school. Michael would take three days of his vacation every week and work weekend days to compensate for the lost time.

We had a plan in place, and all I could do was pray and keep my fingers crossed that nothing would interfere with my rescheduled radiation dates.

Chapter 23

"Kids, let's go!" I directed my voice up the stairs.

Michael poured himself a cup of coffee from the coffee bar into a travel mug, and I pulled my sneakers on as the kids shuffled to the front door.

"I'm ready," Robbie said. He carried a small backpack filled with his bathing suit and iPad. Alex ran into the mudroom, searching for her shoes.

"Time to go." I held open the door, and all three of my family members exited the house in single file. I checked to make sure all the lights were off, and the home security system was on.

We climbed into the Range Rover and headed over to Jessica's house.

"I expect you to be on your best behavior," I said to them. "Try to stay six feet apart and wear your masks, especially if you get closer than that. I know it feels silly, but we need to be safe."

Robbie rolled his eyes.

"If you go in the pool, take your masks off, but be aware of how close you are to each other. We will be back in a few hours."

"Do we have to wear masks? What if Malia isn't wearing a mask?" Robbie asked.

"I expect you to use your best judgment. The state mandate is wearing a mask and staying six feet apart. I expect you to try your best to adhere to those rules."

Chapter 23

"What are you doing today?" asked Alex, staring out the window.

"Today, I meet with the doctor, and then they are going to do a test to look at my brain, and then they are going to make a special mask that I can wear during radiation," I explained. I wasn't sure if that was right, but it sounded good, and it matched what I found on the internet.

Michael drove us across town to Jessica's, and we quickly exchanged pleasantries and farewells before hopping in the car for the first of many commutes to the radiation department.

Due to the pandemic, Michael had to be registered at the front desk by Dr. Landry. We took off our masks from home, put on a hospital mask, signed into the information booth, and headed to his office.

Dr. Landry's nurse greeted us in the lobby and escorted to his office. Dr. Landry sat in a rolling office chair and rolled between his desk and couch. He stood up to greet us and then sat down again, waving toward the sofa for Michael and me to sit. His nurse stood behind him, gathering paperwork and consent forms for us to sign.

"Your tumor is easy," he said, with an air of arrogance. "It will take twenty-five visits. You'll get zapped three times each day from three different angles. We'll meet in a year for a follow-up MRI to make sure it hasn't grown."

I thought we would have done an MRI sooner because my tumor was two millimeters from my optic nerve and still growing.

What if the radiation didn't work? What if he was zapping me in all the wrong places? I didn't understand or fully trust his recommendation, but I told myself that he was the expert and who was I to question him?

Dr. Landry continued, "You might feel fatigued but nothing else. You are young and healthy. We have a 90% chance you will never need another surgery or treatment. We wouldn't be doing this if we thought it wouldn't work. Do you have any questions?"

I looked at Michael, realizing how unprepared I was for this appointment. Dr. Landry believed twenty-five days of radiation would kill the tumor. I shoved the million questions as far from my mind as possible.

"This here is a waiver," he said, rolling over to the couch.

The two sheets of paper sat across my lap as I flipped back and forth.

"Some potential outcomes could be further eye damage, loss of pituitary function, brain cancer, hair loss, and scalp sensitivity." He pointed at the line for me to sign.

"Brain cancer?" I asked, alarmed.

"Yeah, it's extremely rare. One out of five hundred," he replied.

I must have heard him wrong. *One out of five hundred could get brain cancer?* I tried to rationalize my fear, wondering just how many people had the same tumor with my exact treatment plan, and decided that I had to be one of the four hundred ninety-nine that didn't get it.

"What does a loss of pituitary function mean?" I asked.

"That means your pituitary gland will die. Your thyroid and adrenal will also die. It will take between three and five years for things to be affected fully. You don't want to have more kids, do you?" he asked.

I shook my head no and quickly signed the paper without really reading or understanding what it said.

He sent us across the hospital to have another CT scan done for mapping purposes.

"Do you know what is happening right now?" the technician asked as I moved into a room away from the waiting room.

"Not really," I said.

"Did Dr. Landry explain what we were doing today?" she asked again.

"Um, no." I lay down on the table.

"We are making your radiation mask today. We're going to place this sheet of plastic over your face and mold it. It's going to feel warm and wet." She held up a rectangular piece of stiff cream plastic that had crosshatches from top to bottom. "Then we are going to secure it to the table and put stickers on it to assist with the mapping. It will take about twenty minutes or so for your mask to dry."

Three more technicians came into the room.

"Close your eyes," someone said.

Suddenly, I felt warm, damp pressure on my face. Everything felt wet. Multiple hands pressed on my face, pushing and rubbing the plastic so it molded into every crevice of my face.

Chapter 23

Rub-Rub-Rub. Press-Press-Press. Push-Push-Push.

They pulled the plastic down and snapped it to the table below me. I struggled to breathe and couldn't move any muscles in my face.

As the face mask dried, they pulled me in and out of the CT-Scan machine taking photos. My mobility decreased, and I couldn't open my eyes. I tried, but my eyelids wouldn't budge. Every time I swallowed, my lower jaw pushed against the hard plastic, digging under my chin.

I thought about a time when I was happy and when life wasn't quite so complicated. In my mind, I saw the dim ambiance from candles, heard soothing instrumental music, and smelled the aromatherapy diffusing into the air.

That pressure on my eyeballs? Those were cool cucumber slices laying on my eyes to prevent puffiness. That pressure on my face? That was a peel-away mask removing all the impurities of my skin and my life.

I transported myself to a different place to take away my discomfort, and it worked.

They wheeled me out of the machine and removed the mask

"When you are all done with radiation, you can take this home with you and run it over with your car," the radiation technician said with enthusiasm. I smiled at her, and she added, "People do it all the time."

I thought about what she said on the drive home from the hospital. "Michael." I turned to him. "Is this a big deal? I feel like I keep getting mixed messages."

"What do you mean?" he asked, merging onto the highway.

"Well, Dr. Walker said that she got two-thirds of it out, but Dr. Chalksky said that if I didn't have radiation, I would go blind and die. Then, Dr. Landry said it's a no-big-deal tumor, yet there is a one in five hundred chance I will get brain cancer, and the radiation technician told me to run over my mask with my car."

We sat in silence for a few moments, and I giggled. This whole situation felt so absurd. "I don't know how I am supposed to feel. It's mixed messages, and sometimes I feel okay with everything, and other times I feel overwhelmed by how much I don't understand."

"Ash, what you have might be common in the head tumor world, but it's not common in real life. I think they live for this stuff, and they work on it every day. To them, it's not that big of a deal, but it could be catastrophic to us. It completely rocked our world upside down. It's a big deal, yes. You are getting radiation into your head which is where your brain is. It is absolutely a big deal, and you have every right to feel overwhelmed. But it's not cancer, and we are so thankful for that. By it not being cancer, you don't have that added stress of cancer killing you. But just because it's benign doesn't mean it won't change your life or your health. So feel what you need to feel. Whatever you feel is right. And it is okay if what you feel changes. No one is going through this except for you."

I sat in silence, thinking about his words. I still couldn't believe that it had been nine months since our world flipped on its side.

This was the final chapter in our pituitary story, and I was determined to make it end on a happy note.

Chapter 24

The night before my first radiation treatment, I couldn't sleep. I was nervous but not as panicky as I was before my surgeries a few months back. When my surgeries occurred, I was scared that I would die and leave my children motherless. For radiation, I was nervous about going to a hospital every day during a pandemic and bringing home unwanted germs. Thankfully, my family was generally healthy, but the anxiety was still there.

I sat at the kitchen table and pulled out our old photo albums while sipping on a cup of chamomile tea. The dim light over the stove and sink wasn't enough to see the photos' fine details, so I turned on the bright overhead light that Michael had replaced two years prior.

When I had convinced myself that I had Seasonal Affect Disorder, I told Michael I needed brighter lights in our home because it was just too dark and depressing with our lightbulbs. I sent him out to Home Depot, and he returned with daytime LED lights that practically buzzed with electricity when they were on. The lights were so bright, it was painful for my family to look at them, but at the time, the difference was minuscule for me.

Now, sitting at the island with photos strewn about, the lights felt appropriate. They didn't hurt my eyes, and they helped me see the angle of the tabletop, the colors in the kitchen backsplash, and the fine lines and color hue differences within the photographs.

I pulled out an album from before we were married. The photos were a disorganized mix of holidays, apartment life, and family. I piled them and flipped through, smiling at the memories.

One particular photo showed the two of us after we moved into our first apartment. In the background, I saw the futon Jason, Tiffany, and Amanda had purchased for us as a housewarming gift. We had a boxy television that sat on an upside down Rubbermaid tote and another upside down Rubbermaid tote acting as a coffee table in front of the futon.

Jason, Melinda, Michael, and I had squeezed into the futon. I had just gotten a new camera with a timer, and we were messing around with the settings. In the photo, I looked at the others. It looked like I was scolding them for not being ready, which was ironic because they were all smiling, and I was the one who looked miserable. My wide mouth, furrowed eyebrows, and hands up in the air exclaimed disdain. The other three grinned and leaned onto each other and away from me.

Although representing a happy memory, this photo saddened me because I recognized the unhappy person I was. I always needed to control all situations, and this photo summed up my life. I was so busy holding the reins of the moments that made life enjoyable that I missed the opportunity to enjoy the moment. I turned the photo upside down and slid it into the album jacket at the end of the book.

The next photo I picked up was of Michael, the kids, and myself standing on the front stoop of our current house. Robbie was five, and Alex was three. Violets poked beside the bushes next to the porch. The healthy, green grass was soft enough to ditch the shoes, and the windows glistened. Our younger, enthusiastic selves stood together on the steps of our dream home.

After the kids were born, I went back to work as quickly as I could. The days were long, but I knew that I needed to work hard and long to give the kids what they deserved. Most days, I didn't take a lunch break and continued to plug away at my projects. When Alex was two, they promoted me to Project Manager, and with that came a substantial raise. I knew that if I kept working, they would recognize my efforts.

Gramma had passed away a few months before Alex was born, which

Chapter 24

devastated me. First my parents, then Grampy, and now Gramma, and I was only twenty-nine. Feeling abandoned, I leaned into Michael.

I wasn't ready to be on my own. I relied heavily on Jason and Michael to get me through the grieving process. That first year without her was a time filled with tears. I wasn't crying for her only; I was shedding pain and loss for my parents as well.

Looking back, I recognized how their deaths taught me how to survive tough times, like this past year.

A few months after Gramma passed, I got a certified letter in the mail from a lawyer in Boston. My grandmother's sister, who was still alive, had been holding onto their will for years. I guess my Gramma and Grampa didn't trust Jason or me with such an important document, or they didn't want to burden us.

My grandparents had invested in the stock market back in the 1980s when Microsoft was a new company. Grampy wasn't a risk taker, especially when it came to money. I was surprised he would invest, but was thankful that he did.

The lawyer notified Jason and me that we could cash out the stocks or keep them in the stock market, but the stocks were ours. Michael and I decided to cash out some of the stocks to help with the down payment on a "forever" home for our kids.

We couldn't afford the house we wanted, but we told ourselves we could. The bank encouraged us to get pre-approved for the maximum amount our income allowed, but the banks didn't factor in the level of debt and the total amount of minimum payments to other accounts we had to dole out each month.

"Michael!" I remembered saying, short of breath, staring at the house for sale. "This place is stunning!" My eyes sparkled in awe, and I grabbed onto his hand, communicating my utter love for the cathedral ceilings, updated kitchen, and soaking tub with a separate shower in the master bathroom.

"This house," our Realtor began, "was built in 1850 but was completely gutted and rebuilt to attract the modern-day family. The original fireplace is still intact." She led us into the formal living room. "The original pine floors have been refinished." She showcased the floor below with her arm, waving from side to side. "The doors all have the original doorknobs," she added, pointing to the sparkly crystal knobs.

"Michael," I whispered. I didn't need to say more.

"The house has three bedrooms, three bathrooms, a formal living room, formal dining room, eat-in kitchen, and great room. The great room has cathedral ceilings. There is brand new plumbing, electrical, and roof," Anna ticked off the bullet points in the listing.

I was in love with the character, charm, and modern conveniences. I saw this deep red brick house, and I knew we needed this house. There was plenty of room, and we could stay forever.

The problem was that it was at the top of our price range. Well, not even our price range, but our pre-approved loan amount. Anna, our Realtor, convinced me that we needed it, so I convinced Michael, and Michael tried to talk some sense into me, but it didn't work. I knew I had worked hard enough to earn this home, and we deserved it.

Looking at this picture now, I recognized the pure amazement and excitement in my eyes. I realized the reservation behind Michael's smile and apprehension behind his eyes.

The kids would have been happy in a cardboard box. They had sat in the grass in front of us on the steps, Alex wailing and Robbie throwing grass clippings at her.

At the time, this house was the pinnacle of my success as a person. It defined who I was as a contributing member of society.

Now, I sipped my tea and took in the granite countertops and stainless steel appliances. I wondered how something so physical became so important. Obsessed with working my life away so that we could "afford" nice things, I never had time to enjoy them. This entire house for so many years was just for show, and if I were honest with myself, my children were part of the performance.

I thought about what our life would have been like had I been satisfied with what God had given us. We had two beautiful children, and I barely knew them because I chose never to be home.

Chapter 24

What if I had stayed home with them when they were toddlers? What if we lived in a modest home or, God-forbid, lived in an apartment? What if my main focus was family instead of work?

Right now, I've been out of work for nine months. I hadn't been checking emails, working on projects, or having any communication with my team except to say that I was extending my leave. Nine long months and work was still working, but it was working without me. I always thought work couldn't function without me or my spreadsheets, but I learned through absence that I wasn't the answer to all work-related problems. Never in my life had I realized just how disposable I was, even though I gave up everything for their paycheck and promotions.

My work had excellent health insurance, which is why Michael and I had not gone entirely bankrupt after my diagnosis. I thought about life and God and money and family and work and realized that timing is everything.

With only eight to ten years left before my kids left the house for good, I couldn't allow myself to miss out on those ten years like I did the last. I couldn't go back to the mundane, obligatory marriage we had been holding onto for the sake of love, kids, and money. I knew that once this health disaster was over and our insurance covered all my treatments, I was going to make a change and finally put our family first.

I realized that it is great to love things, like our house, but things never loved you back. The most important part of life was family, and they stuck by me through this entire disaster. I owed it to them to put them first.

Sadly, I put the photos away, realizing that if I looked closely, we weren't happy. People from the outside may have seen us and thought, "Gee, I want to be like them," but I knew that we were living a façade. I was living a façade, and Michael was coasting along with me because he loved me. I wasn't sure if it was comfort, consistency, loyalty, or love that had kept him by my side all those years, but I knew that he deserved more. I decided I would finish my treatment out strong, reconnect with my family, and never go back to how we were or who I was.

I turned off all the lights, put the albums away, and crept upstairs to bed. I snuggled up against Michael and felt his heartbeat through my cheek. I breathed in his neck and kissed his shoulder.

Life was funny sometimes. It kicked you down when you least expected it but helped you up once you learned the lesson. I closed my eyes, knowing morning would come too quickly.

Chapter 25

It was my first day at the radiation clinic. Due to the coronavirus, Michael was unable to enter the hospital with me. I checked into the main reception area, where they gave me a new face mask, checked my name and appointment, and walked me through the hospital maze of hallways, elevators, and stairwells. I walked into another waiting area and checked in for my appointment.

When it was my turn, the radiation technician walked me down another corridor and into a large white room with a narrow black table in the center. I lay down on the table, and one of the many women in the room explained that they would be doing some measurements and position me correctly for all the treatment angles. They explained that the first appointment would take longer than most, and typically I would be in and out in twenty minutes.

As thankful as I was that the appointment would take only twenty minutes, I was disappointed to miss so much of my summer driving back and forth every day. I wondered what my children were doing at that moment.

I had an absolute number of treatments, so after today, I only had twenty-four to go. I lay down on my back with a warm, toasty blanket pulled up over my legs and torso. I tried to melt into the table and relax my body, but it was too hard and narrow.

"You ready?" I heard a voice ask from behind me.

I nodded and felt the plastic mask encapsulate my head and pull me down as they snapped the mask into place. Click-click-click-click-click-click.

"You okay?"

I tried to speak, but my mask stabilized my closed mouth, and I couldn't move my lips. I tried to give a thumbs up instead, but my hands remained hidden under the blanket. My eyes gently pressed down, and I struggled to swallow. They explained that they were marking up my mask to ensure a proper position. Before every radiation angle, they took a mini-CT scan to ensure I was in the correct position.

I heard machine noises and felt like I was swaying back and forth in a hammock. I wasn't sure if I was moving or if the room was moving, and my equilibrium shifted. The technicians explained that we were sharing the radiation beam with another room, so we had to wait to continue.

I listened to Billy Joel over the loudspeaker, focusing on the beat of the music, unable to move my head. I wondered if the CT machine could sense my brain dancing with the music, so I tried to hold still. Now and then, I heard what sounded like a giant camera shutter next to my ear, and flash of light bounced behind my eyelids. Sometimes the light was directly above me, and other times it was straight to the side.

Someone spoke a series of words, letters, and numbers: 82.80-30.Shifter-A2.Snout-16 Gantry.

I had no idea what the sequence meant, but I had a feeling it was essential to the accuracy of what was about to happen. A voice behind my head, changing equipment and calling out numbers and letters was followed by a voice repeating the same numbers and letters further away.

"Okay, we will be right back." There was just me and Billy Joel. Him singing over the loudspeaker and me singing in my head. I didn't hear the machine move, turn on, or turn off.

I lay there, trying not to swallow, pretending that I was getting another facial, and wondered how much longer it would take until I could leave.

What would happen if I sneezed? Would the radiation shoot into my brain? My eyes? Would I die because the mask was so tight on my face and bolted to the table that I would concuss myself by the force of the sneeze?

My nose itched, but I couldn't reach it. I pretended that my hands scratched

Chapter 25

it, and the itch went away.

I heard doors open and voices slowly increase in volume. "Okay, one down, two more to go."

In the middle of my third angle, the group of technicians left the room and returned a few minutes later. "Hi, Ashley, we're here. We had to call an Engineer because the cable broke. It's no problem. The Engineers are next door. It will be a few minutes."

I tried to respond but couldn't move my mouth behind what felt like saran wrap over my face. Instead, I waited. I heard movement all around me but couldn't place who it was or what was happening. It sounded like someone was directly over my face, changing the equipment.

After the engineer left, we had to wait for the laser machine to become available again. I lay on the table, trying my hardest to move my mind away from radiation and back to the sauna.

When they lifted my mask off my face, over sixty minutes had passed. "Wow, that mask was tight," one woman said. "It'll go away in a few hours. Sorry for the delay. You did great! We will see you tomorrow."

I grabbed my things and headed out to the elevator. I passed a mirror and saw my face, imprinted like a waffle. Small, swollen diamond shapes pressed my nose from the crisscross design on the mask.

I climbed into the car next to Michael and apologized for taking so long.

"It's fine! I've been sitting here, catching up on YouTube videos. I talked to Jess, and she brought the kids back to our house because Robbie forgot to pack a change of clothes for after swimming."

We made our way out of the parking garage and onto the Pike. I couldn't wait to get home and rest. I hadn't done much the past hour, but my body felt like it had been run over.

My imprinted forehead was still present when we got home an hour and a half later.

"Hey, Mom," Robbie greeted me. I hugged him, and he said, "How do you make a waffle smile?" His gaze rose to my imprinted forehead.

I had never been good at telling or understanding jokes, so I shrugged my shoulders. "I don't know. Tell me." My head couldn't come up with a witty response.

"You butter him up!"

I giggled because he was so darn funny. *When did he become this comical?* "Did you make that up?" I asked, taking off my shoes so the hospital germs wouldn't leave the entryway.

"Kind of. What happened to your face?" he asked.

"The radiation mask is tight. I hope it isn't like that every day." I rubbed my forehead, feeling the pressed grooves.

Michael kissed me and said, "You look beautiful."

I smiled at him.

Alex stood in the doorway between the foyer and the kitchen and looked at me, unsure what to do.

"Hi, Alex," I said, stretching my arms to her. She awkwardly came over and gave me a gentle hug.

"I missed you," she said and then bounded into the great room to watch a Disney movie. I decided to approach her again when the swelling in my face went down.

"Jessica?" I called into the kitchen.

She stuck her head out of the door frame and waved. "Welcome home. How was it?" She approached and hesitated, appearing unsure if she should give me a hug or a fist bump due to my medical stuff, being at the hospital, and recommended coronavirus precautions.

I gave her my elbow to rub in greeting. "It was bizarre. They snapped my head to the table. I couldn't open my eyes, I couldn't talk, and I couldn't swallow. It lasted over an hour, and the machine broke in the middle of it. At one point, my anxiety was going, and I started to panic that we would have a fire alarm pulled and no one would unsnap my head."

Jessica's eyes got wide. "Really?"

I nodded.

"I'm sure if the hospital were on fire, someone would remember you. I know they wouldn't leave you. What's up with your face?" She got close to my forehead, looking at the design staring back at her.

"The mask. It was so tight it was cutting off circulation in my face." I

Chapter 25

shrugged and grinned, not really sure if what I said was accurate, but it made sense to me.

"Wow! That is so crazy. I am glad you're home," she said, strutting into the kitchen. "Dinner is cooking. It should be ready around five. The kids just had a snack, and Robbie did some of his summer reading already. He's playing video games with his friends. Malia and Alex just started watching Hamilton, so you probably have an hour or so before the kids need you."

I loved having Jessica nearby to help us. Having Jessica was like having a roommate. She knew my kids well enough to anticipate their needs, and knew what they liked and didn't like to eat. She didn't have to entertain them every second of the day. She was an extension of our family.

She did her thing in our kitchen and headed home when it was comfortable for everyone.

"Thank you so much for everything. You have no idea how much you saved me this summer," I said.

Jessica waved her hands at me as if to say, "No big deal," and went into the great room to collect her daughter.

"Tomorrow, we'll bring the kids to you. We should only be gone a few hours. We'll drop them off at ten-thirty." I reiterated.

"Perfect, thanks."

It appeared that we put together a well-oiled machine with a thought through plan to knock this tumor out.

The following days were long and mundane. Wake up, hang out with the kids, drop them off at Jessica's, head to Boston, get my head zapped, come home, pick up the kids, and have dinner together. Every day my time was different, so we never created an actual routine around these appointments.

We tried to create positive memories on the weekends because that was the only uninterrupted time we had as a family. Still, our options were limited due to the pandemic and trying to isolate from people. We created a Weekend Bucket List that would have been great family bonding experiences at a different time, but we couldn't do them this year. Beach, lake, shopping, out to dinner, and miniature golf were all off the table.

We knew the kids were bored, and I tried my hardest not to feel guilty about it.

It is one summer with extenuating circumstances. Next year will be different.

We did what we could to make our home exciting. We bought a slip-n-slide for the backyard, cooked on the grill as much as we could, and played board games at least twice a week. We contemplated getting a puppy but decided it would set us up for failure, not knowing what time I had to be in the city each day.

"Mom?" Alex called into our great room. Asleep on the couch with an afghan made by my grandmother thrown over my legs, I opened one eye to see her standing in the door. I had just finished my third week of radiation, and the fatigue was setting in sporadically. I found that some days I became the energizer bunny, bouncing from one cleaning task to the next, while the next day, I resembled a sack of potatoes, barely able to get myself off the couch to grab a snack.

I watched her her tiptoe in, trying not to wake me with the click-clack of her shoes on the hardwood floor. "I'm up," I groaned, pushing myself up into a seated position. I tapped the cushion next to me, inviting her to sit. "How are you?"

Alex smiled at me, batting her nonexistent eyelashes, trying to be extra sweet. "Malia got a kitten yesterday," she started. "She's adorable."

Yes, I had heard about this kitten. Jessica's coworker lived on a farm, and her barn cat had kittens. Jessica stopped at the farm store with Malia for fresh vegetables, and the kittens climbed over each other in a box in the corner, meowing and peeking their head over the edge. Jessica didn't want a kitten, but Malia fell in love, and the guilt of having a "No-Fun" summer pushed her to take a kitten home.

"Yes, I heard. What is her name?" I asked.

"Malia wanted the kitten to remind her of this summer, so she named it Tina. For quarantine."

I chuckled because that was a creative and appropriate name.

"Mom, can we get a kitten?"

I sat there for a moment before responding, trying to process her question and organize my answer. My brain had been resembling an internet

Chapter 25

connection from dial-up days, and my kids knew that I needed at least five seconds to process and answer simple questions.

Alex waited and didn't break eye contact.

"Well, I don't know if that would be a great idea. We don't have a lot of time to take care of an animal," I replied.

"Please, Mom? I will take care of it. I can use my allowance money to feed it if you want me to. I will keep it in my room at night, so you don't have to take care of it. I'll even change its litter box if you teach me how."

I appreciated the gesture, but I knew that I would be cleaning the litter box if we got a kitten. It was clear Alex had been practicing her debating skills before she came down to speak to me. I loved her perseverance and determination when she pushed for something, especially something she loved.

How can I say no?

The kids had been stuck at home for six months, we hadn't eaten out, gone to the movies, or the beach all summer. We were stuck in the house on a good day, and on a bad day, I shuttled them around for a few hours to go to my appointments at the hospital.

My brain reverted to my pre-tumor thinking: cats scratch furniture, they smell, they cost money, and they make a mess. I shook my head to get those negative thoughts out of my head and instead flipped my perspective.

We are living in a pandemic. Who exactly am I cleaning this house for? Why do I care about scratch marks on our leather couch? Does it matter?

I rubbed my temples and forehead, feeling a headache building. "Did you ask Dad?" I asked.

"Yes, he said to ask you," Alex said.

"Sure. Why not?" Of course, Michael said to ask me. He didn't want to be the bad guy, and I couldn't be the bad guy in this situation. I wasn't the cause for the pandemic, but I was the cause for interrupting their days this summer.

Alexandria clapped her hands in excitement and gave me a big hug. It was the first genuine hug I had received in months from her. That hug had enough love and affection to fill my heart with gratitude for my family and keep it full all day. I started to wonder what lessons this summer was teaching my kids, and I hoped it taught them that families stuck together no matter what.

"Robbie!" Alex screamed, running out of the room. "Dad! Robbie! Mom said yes."

Robbie didn't acknowledge her, but Michael handed her his cell phone and told her to Face Time Malia to tell her the good news. As much as I didn't want a kitten under my feet, keeping me up at night, knocking things off my dresser, and ripping up the curtains, I knew that Alex had had a tough year, and if this made her year a tiny bit better, it was worth it.

The next day, we picked up Llama, our newest family member. Llama was white and fluffy with blue eyes, and she looked like a princess. I imagined her groomed with a pink bow in her hair and understood why she was a perfect companion for Alex.

Robbie picked out a fluffy white kitten with a black spot on and under its tail and asked if he could bring it home. Although Robbie wasn't excited about the kitten when Alex told him I said yes, he couldn't stop himself from getting giddy when he held the kittens at the farm store. He explained that we should never separate family members, and I agreed.

Not only did we get Llama, but we also got Llama's brother, Fuzzbutt. I wasn't too excited about the name, but he was Robbie's, and Robbie was an eleven-year-old boy. I called Fuzzbutt "Fuzzy," and Robbie didn't seem to notice.

The happy kids played with their new friends, which distracted them from my situation. In this lonely pandemic, we all needed a special someone to lean on. I had Michael. Robby had Fuzzy, and Alex had Llama.

Our family of four had just grown to six.

Chapter 26

School was starting soon, and no one knew what was happening. The coronavirus was still raging around the country, and states were fumbling to open their businesses safely. Michael had been working non-stop on weekends and evenings, trying to get things organized for the possible reopening of schools.

"What do you think is going to happen?" I asked him over lunch one afternoon.

Alex complained about missing her friends, and she wanted to meet her new teacher. Robbie was moving to the middle school, where he would adjust to new teachers, new rules, and new administration. I tried to tell them that school this year was not going to feel or look the same, regardless of whether it occurred at home or in the building.

Michael shrugged. "I don't know. We're planning and acting like we're reopening, so we've been investigating hand sanitizer stations, fogging machines, and reminder stickers to socially distance. There's a chance all of this stress and money is for nothing, but maybe it'll work."

I kissed him on the lips and thanked him for all the hard work he had put in while also shuttling me around the city.

"If the kids don't go back to school, what am I going to do?" I told work I would return by mid September, about one month after my radiation ended. I didn't think the Human Resources representative believed me because this was the third restart date I had given her since my diagnosis.

"I have a feeling they will go back," Michael said. "If they don't? We'll figure it out."

I thought about the kids not returning to school and how devastating it would be to Alex. Robbie had X-box, which allowed him to communicate with his friends sporadically throughout the pandemic, but Alex relied on her toys for entertainment. She missed the playground and the monkey bars most. My heart fell, knowing that the monkey bars may not be available at recess, and if they were, she would have to stay six feet away from her friends. And, she would huff and puff through a cloth mask when using them.

I dreamed about having an excuse not to go back to work. Not just an excuse, but a valid reason, such as, "Sorry, I need to stay home and educate my children."

I never shared this thought with Michael because our roles had always been me as the breadwinner and the one whose number one priority was work, while his role was to make enough money for eating out, going to the movies, and buying new clothes for the kids. My job paid the bills, and his job paid for the fun stuff.

We had been living on half our income for almost ten months, and we were making it work, but severing my chance at returning to work could be enough to bankrupt us. Plus, the unemployment rate was sky high right now, with all the states shut down. I couldn't imagine purposefully leaving my job when so many people were desperate to work.

That day, they canceled my radiation appointment because the machine broke, and the engineer couldn't fix it in time for my visit. The secretary at the front desk called and left a message.

Disappointed my treatments extended one day further, I was happy to have a day off with my husband. Even though we were supposed to be on the road by now, I called Jessica and asked if we could drop the kids off for a few hours as planned. She agreed and I promised I would make it up to her.

Guilt for sending them to someone else's house because I wanted to spend alone time with my husband slid into my mind, but I reminded myself that couples had to sacrifice to strengthen their marriages.

Chapter 26

Alex and Robbie didn't appear fazed when we said goodbye. They had already raced into Malia's room to play with the kitten.

When we got home, Michael asked, "How long do we have before we have to pick up the kids?"

I took a sip of cold coffee and said in the sexiest voice I could muster, "Three hours. Do you want to play a game?" I tried to look seductive, but I knew sexy and flirty were not things my body did well. Feeling frisky, I giggled and whispered in his ear, "I have a game for you."

I traipsed up the stairs, looking over my shoulder to see if he was following me.

"Sit down," I instructed in my most teacher-like voice. "On the floor," I clarified.

"What game are we playing?" Michael sat on the floor with his legs outstretched, leaning back on his arms, waiting for the next direction. I could see the curiously flickering behind his eyes.

I grabbed a deck of cards and sat across from him, dealing out some cards between the two of us. "Strip poker."

He looked at me with lust behind his eyes and a secret on his lips.

I felt like I had lost my mind. I didn't know who this person was, and I probably hadn't seen this person for close to twenty years. Had the tumor been pushing on my brain to the point where my vulnerability was depleted? Now that the tumor was gone, I was back, and I was not backing down.

"I'm down," Michael said, giddy with anticipation.

We played round after round of Texas Hold'em, slowly stripping away our clothes, fears, and disappointment in the life we had been living.

"Michael," I said as we lay in bed, warmth glowing from his body and into mine. "Did you ever imagine we would be here?"

"No. As hard as it was, I'm glad it happened. I feel whole again. I feel loved and appreciated and wanted. I don't think this closeness or this connection would have happened without your major health scare."

I agreed that the tumor had changed me and had changed us. We faced the terror of me leaving him to be a single father, muddling through parenthood alone. We met the realization that things and tangible items did not equate to love or happiness. Our children were growing up, and I recognized how much I had missed.

This tumor slapped me across the face and shook me, demanding I wake up.

"I have fallen back in love with you," I said, staring into his eyes. "I have fallen back in love with the life we created together. I'm sorry if I ever made you feel like you weren't enough."

Michael had never uttered the sentiment that I made him feel unworthy, but looking back on the past ten years, I could see how my obsession with meeting the American expectation of what success looked like could have made him feel inferior.

"I love the fact that you're content with what we have, and you aren't chasing the carrot to fit the narrative of what I fed ourselves our entire marriage. I admire you for standing by your beliefs. I wish I were more like you."

Michael didn't respond to my monologue. He stared at the ceiling, thinking about my words, actions, and the course life had taken us. He kissed my forehead and held me tighter.

***

Ten days later, I went to the hospital for my last scheduled treatment. At this point, the process ended in one fell swoop. I entered the room, lay on the bed, and closed my eyes. The mask came on, photographs clicked, and I heard a string of numbers and words. People exited the room, came back, and took my mask off. The first day it took over an hour, and the last day it took less than twenty minutes.

I approached the chair where my pocketbook, mask, and jacket sat and found a laminated certificate of completion with my name, the date, and the technician's names.

As I read the words related to courage, perseverance, and good health, I started to cry. I never realized how much pent-up emotion I carried deep within my soul. I had been on an emotional rollercoaster that traveled from fear to worry to pain to laughter to appreciation to satisfaction, and I was finally ready to get off the ride. The finality of the experience hit me. I never

Chapter 26

thought I would finish.

The technicians walked me out of the room to a short hallway with a bell secured to the wall. Underneath the bell was a plaque that read: **Ring this bell three times well-It's toll will clearly say-My treatments are done-This course has run-And now I'm on my way**.

I gave the technician my phone, sad that Michael couldn't be there to witness such a milestone achievement, and asked her to video and take photos of me marking this monumental race in my life. Even though my face mask hid my happiness, I had a massive smile on my face. I rang the bell loud and clear with assertion.

The staff members erupted in applause, and I rode the elevator up to the main floor for the very last time. This chapter was finally over.

IV

Epilogue

Not all storms come to disrupt your life. Some come to clear your path.
—Paulo Coelho

12 Months Later

"What was I doing?" I asked Robbie, quickly scanning the kitchen. Robbie rolled his eyes at me. "Mom, you said you were going to start dinner." He took a sip of lemonade and waited to ensure that I followed through on my earlier directive.

I opened the refrigerator and pulled out the chicken tenders. "That's right," I said with a chuckle. "Chicken tenders, fries, and corn. Coming right up." I continued to chuckle to myself because I forgot something as easy as dinner. Again.

My short-term memory hadn't recovered from radiation, but of course my doctor said that it wasn't from the tumor or the treatments. It could have been the constant change in hormone levels, but no one seemed to have a definitive reason. When I couldn't function in the way I used to, I went for more labs and medication adjustments. I would be on complete hormone replacement within five years, so I figured my flightiness was par for the course.

I used to get upset that my brain no longer worked the way it had before. I tried many strategies to remember: writing it down, repeating it to myself, completing a task before getting distracted by something else, but it never seemed to help. Now, one year later, I needed to accept that I was no longer Ashley Martin, Queen of Multitasking and Productivity. I honestly was a space cadet.

Robbie went upstairs to his room, and I got to work. "Dinner. Dinner. Dinner," I said to myself. I wrote the word DINNER on the dry erase board next to our refrigerator and placed all the ingredients I needed on the counter.

Partway through cooking, Michael came into the kitchen and wrapped his arms around me, giving me a tight squeeze. He kissed me on the cheek and asked how long until dinner was ready. "Thirty minutes," I said, glancing at the timer on the stove. He headed off to his workshop to tinker with his wood burning kit.

"Mom!" Alex hollered down the stairs. "I need you!" Her shrill voice pierced through me as only a true emergency could.

I ran up the stairs, wondering what the crisis was. Alex stood in the bathroom over the vanity staring at herself in the mirror. Her face was ashen, and her eyes were wide. She held scissors in her hand, suspended over the sink. Looking down, I saw the sink basin coated in hair.

"Oh, Alex!"

Above her eyebrows, I saw two inches of forehead, and above that was a jagged, crooked line of dark hair cascading toward the top of her right ear. Laughter filled my belly and rose through my chest. It threatened to break beyond my windpipe, but I stuffed it down. I fought the urge to burst out in giggles, and instead busied myself with cleaning up the hair.

A dam of wetness quivered behind her eyes. They burst and gushed down her cheeks, and she sobbed at her reflection.

I quickly grabbed her, pulled her into my shoulder, and silently laughed at the haircut that all girls experimented with before young adulthood. I stroked her hair and whispered, "It's okay. It's only hair. It will grow back."

"I needed a haircut," she said. She was right.

With the pandemic, we tried our hardest to limit face-to-face contact with anyone we didn't know, and haircuts were at the bottom of our priority list.

"Alex," I said, pulling her body away from mine and staring into her face. "You are right. You needed a haircut, but only professionals should cut bangs. No matter what. Bangs are not meant for the average Joe." I giggled again.

"What am I going to do?" she cried, pulling at the uneven, thick and thin bangs dotting her forehead. I grabbed a hat and threw it at her.

"Here. Wear this. No one will notice," I said, mainly thinking about her older brother, who loved to make her life miserable. Alex put it on, and her bangs disappeared.

"Mom?" Robbie yelled up the stairs.

"Up here!" I called back.

"I smell something burning!" he said.

I froze in the bathroom, sniffing the air. I didn't smell anything from where I was.

"Did Dad light a candle?" I called down to him again.

"No, I don't think so. It's coming from the kitchen. Is the chicken done?"

The chicken!

I ran out of the bathroom and down the stairs skipping the last three steps. I bolted into the kitchen, turned the oven off, checked the chicken. Black smoke billowed into our kitchen.

"Open the windows! Open the door!" I screamed to anyone that would listen.

Robbie slowly moved around the house, and I zipped by him, turning on all the ceiling fans.

"Don't tell your father!" I said to Robbie, waving a towel below the smoke detector. Michael already thought I was losing my mind. I didn't need him to know that I was also burning down the house.

I left the oven closed for fifteen minutes before venturing to open it, praying that the smoke would be gone. The hardened, black chicken was inedible. The pan was black, as well. I pulled it out and dropped the pan in the sink.

I cracked up laughing at the absurdity of the day. First, I forgot to start dinner, then Alex's bangs got hacked, and then I forgot to finish dinner. Just a typical day in the Martin household.

I pulled out a bag of Perdue frozen chicken tenders and threw them in the microwave. Twenty minutes later, the original baking dish was cleaned, the burned chicken was down the disposal, and the evidence of my dinner fiasco was gone. I lit a few candles to mask the lingering burning smell that permeated the house.

"Is dinner ready?" Michael asked, popping into the kitchen. I turned and smiled at him with a large, exaggerated grin.

"Mm-hmmm," I nodded, kissing him on the lips and handing him a beer.

"What's that smell?" he asked, looking around suspiciously.

He knows me too well.

"Oh, I don't know. We had the door open, and I think Mr. Carter has a fire going. The smell must have come in from next door," I quickly replied, tossing the bottle opener at him.

"Huh," he said, looking at me. I knew he wanted to challenge me because he had just been outside, but instead, he said, "Dinner looks great."

We sat at the dinner table and chatted about the day. My burned chicken and Alex's bangs never came up in conversation. Alex removed her hat and replaced it with a headband. The boys were oblivious. I winked at Alex when Robbie brought up her greasy hair, and I winked at Robbie when Michael commented on the chicken.

After dinner, the kids went upstairs, and I gave Michael a kiss of gratitude. "Thank you," I said, holding out my beer bottle to clink against his. "Thank you for hanging in with me this year. I know that I'm different. I forget things. I laugh more than I have ever laughed. I probably cry more than I have ever cried too. Overall, I feel more, and I know it must be hard for you to adjust to my constant changes. I love you. I love our family. I love the life we have made and the journey so far. To us." I held up my bottle again. "To another fifty years. To losing our memory together. To keeping it together, together."

We clinked bottles, and I snuggled up against him with the newest photo album I had filled sitting next to me on the table. "Do you want to see the pictures?" I asked, tilting the photo album toward him.

He took the album and opened the cover to flip through the pages. This year, I uploaded all the photos from my phone and printed them. The pictures from the year of my diagnosis were too painful for me to look at, but the transformation observed in the photos from this past year inspired me.

The photo album cover said, "Find joy in the journey," and although most people would agree the year of my diagnosis was the journey, I would argue that the year after was a more significant journey.

During the diagnosis year, we realized the true struggle was making the changes and keeping the changes active within our lives. The battle came down to remembering all we had gone through as a family because we couldn't go back to where we were before that time. I promised myself that I wouldn't go back.

I couldn't return to a life of prioritizing work over family or living under an umbrella of stress because of little things, such as dishes and laundry. I couldn't go back to living under constant micromanagement of the people I loved because it wasn't fair to me, and it wasn't fair to them. I refused to live in a home where I made all the rules and bent the rules for myself but no one else.

I wanted my family to resemble a young willow tree, having their branches bend with the flexibility and uncertainty of life, rather than an oak tree that breaks under the tiniest amount of stress.

We flipped through the album, looking at the journey our family took that first year after my treatments finished. The photos were disproportionately taken in our home rather than in luxurious locations.

I saw pictures of Alex and Robbie making homemade pizza, Michael raking leaves, and Fuzzy and Llama stretched out in the windowsills. I saw photos of our garden, dotted with red, yellow, and green, from all the fruit and vegetables that were ripening. I saw pictures of the homemade birthday cake I made and balloons Michael blew up tied to the dining room table. I noticed scratches on the top of the dining room table, marked up from the kids doing their homework against the grain of the wood because they forgot to place a folder under their worksheets.

Some photos showed the home offices we had created for the kids to complete school from the comfort of our own home. Masks blocked our faces and expressions, but we communicated our emotions through our eyes and eyebrows. Things looked different than they had in the past. We looked happier, living a more authentic life.

I stopped at a picture of the four of us, standing on the front porch of a modest home. Robbie was almost as tall as I was, and Alex was nearly as tall as Robbie. Michael wrapped his arm around my waist and pulled me close to him. There was a sign next to the steps that said, "SOLD!" and unlike the other photograph I had examined last year, I saw satisfaction. The kids looked comfortable leaning against the red door behind us, making silly faces at the camera.

We moved out of our fancy, picturesque farmhouse six months ago. I couldn't wait to get out of there. I had thought that house was my dream house, and anyone who saw our house would immediately wonder what they could do to have a house like ours.

After my treatments, I couldn't stomach the absurdity or inauthenticity of the house. I felt like a fraud, living in something that no longer fit who I was, and I hated living a false narrative.

I decided not to return to work after my treatments. I loved the job itself, but it no longer satisfied me. There was too much pressure to play a specific part and look a particular way, so I convinced Michael that we could make it work without me working sixty hours a week. He was skeptical, but I had the perfect excuse when the schools announced that they were reopening, but we didn't have to return. Using my compromised health as a reason, I agreed to stay home and educate the kids.

We struggled financially from that point forward, and selling our house and downsizing was the only plausible solution. Our house sold within days, and we quickly looked at all the homes on the market that might work. We no longer needed to find the "perfect" house or the "forever" house because a house was just a dwelling.

The important thing was finding a home where we could be happy and comfortable. We found a cozy three-bedroom, one-and-a-half-bath home in the next town over.

Knowing that the kids were already missing their friends but couldn't see them at school anyway, we decided to uproot them and move to a new community. It was a fresh start, all around.

The kids were taken aback by the diminished size of the home, but I promised them they could decorate their room any way they liked. At our old house, their rooms needed to fit the narrative I had created. Alex slept in a Victorian-style room equipped with lace curtains and a canopy bed, and Robbie slept in a traditional room with oak furniture and generic bunk beds.

I no longer needed to control every aspect of their lives, and their individuality was free to bust out at the seams.

In this new home, we somehow managed to make life and our finances work. When people asked what I did for a living, I proudly told them that I was a mother. I was always afraid of being a woman and not showing my worth to society, but being a mother was the most critical job. I was no longer willing to sacrifice my happiness for a job pushed on me by people I didn't know.

My health was stable. I continued to be monitored for my hormones and medicated for what was lacking. My hair stopped falling out, my libido was back, and the headaches were gone. My vision wasn't 100% back to normal, but I figured out how to compensate for any blurriness or double vision I experienced.

My weight never rebounded, but I learned to love my body just as it was. Even though I was curvy, I felt sexy and beautiful whenever I was alone with Michael. I knew that my body went through hell and back and demonstrated just how strong I was. Instead of focusing on the changes as battle wounds, I thought of them as warrior victories. My body told a story, and I didn't want to diminish the memories of what we went through because it made us stronger.

Jessica and I ate breakfast every Saturday over Zoom. I ate in the three-season porch overlooking our wooded backyard, where I could find some privacy to share the events she'd missed. Life was hard during the pandemic, but like my journey throughout my pituitary tumor nightmare, we learned to be flexible and appreciate what we had. I had a best friend who was like a sister to me, and when life returned to normal, I would give her the biggest bear hug to thank her for all she had done throughout the years.

Michael and I were more robust than ever, adjusting to our new life. We never thought we would be here, in a different house, being different parents, closer friends, and more intimate lovers. We were in it together, and Michael showed me how vast his love for me could be when I allowed him to enter my heart fully. During Timmy's havoc in my head, Michael proved to me that his loyalty and love were unrelenting, and he would never leave my side.

I closed the photo album and traced the words on the cover. Find joy in the journey. I understood that our pituitary story was never going to end, and that was a great thing. Our journey told us who we were and what was imperative. Our journey strengthened our

family. We found humor and laughter in the simplest moments and practiced gratitude for all we could have lost but didn't.

Our story brought joy, just like the photo album said, and I had finally grabbed onto the happiness that hid in the depths of despair within our journey.

***

For more information about pituitary tumors and how they impact us, please check out It's All in My Head at https://dl.bookfunnel.com/w59eu2trxc

About the Author

E.D. Hackett lives with her husband, two children, and three fur babies in Massachusetts. She wrote short stories as a child and kept a journal throughout most of her life. She majored in Journalism for a hot second in college and graduated with a Master's degree in Speech-language pathology. E.D. Hackett is an SLP by day and a writer by night.

She hopes to convey themes that are relatable to all women, such as self-acceptance, self-love, trust, and identity.

Edy can be found on Facebook, Instagram, and Goodreads, as well as her website www.edhackettauthor.com

You can connect with me on:

- http://www.edhackettauthor.com
- https://www.facebook.com/edhackettwrites
- https://linktr.ee/Edhackett
- https://www.instagram.com/e.d_hackettwrites
- https://www.payhip.com/edhackettauthor

Subscribe to my newsletter:

- https://www.edhackettauthor.com

Also by E.D. Hackett

E.D. Hackett writes women's fiction with one foot in romance.

An Unfinished Story

Complete strangers. A bustling B&B. Can two women help each other find their dreams?

Boston. Joanie Wilson has played it safe her whole life. But her fifteen years of loyalty to the newspaper seem like they count for nothing when her boss announces the business's impending sale. And though she doesn't really enjoy her job, the frightened reporter fights to save it by accepting a remote assignment to write articles on local flavor.

Block Island, RI. Carly Davis longs to live on her own terms. But with her father deceased and her mother's dementia dominating her world, the gregarious young woman feels trapped into running the family's bed-and-breakfast. So when a desperate journalist arrives and swaps her rent for assistance with the property, Carly seizes the chance to finally take a deep breath.

As Joanie becomes immersed in the relaxed atmosphere and meets a handsome police officer, she wonders if her need for safety is costing her happiness. And as Carly grows close to her big-city tenant, she sees a new future opening before her.

Will this accidental friendship trigger the changes both women crave?

An Unfinished Story is the charming first book in The Block Island Saga women's fiction series. If you like relatable characters, sweet romances, and beautiful settings, then you'll love E.D. Hackett's escape to paradise.

Hope Hanna Murphy

She sacrificed too much for them. When her real ancestry shatters her world, will she ever reclaim happiness?

Carly Davis was sure getting away from the island would help. Elated after finally freeing herself from running her late family's inn, her fresh start in Maine fizzles in the aftermath of a failed relationship. And her luck sours further still when an innocent DNA test reveals at least one of her parents had been deceiving her for decades.

Furious she gave up the best years of her life to support people she wasn't even related to, the distraught woman returns home to seek answers about her actual origins. But with her dear friend's sister marrying a guy who is suddenly Carly's cousin, the angry adoptee fears the truth could leave her more alone than ever…

Will she find the joy she so desperately craves, or will her true heritage only bring new sorrow?

Hope Hanna Murphy is the enchanting second book in The Block Island Saga women's fiction series. If you like optimistic stories, conflicted characters, and the strength of community, then you'll love E.D. Hackett's tale of courage.

Reinventing Amara Leventis

She wants everyone to think she's got it together. So where did it all fall apart?

Providence, RI. Amara Leventis craves validation. So when her best friend and roomie gets engaged, the twenty-five-year-old single girl fears she's losing her soulmate… and her apartment forever. Reeling from the sense of abandonment, Amara turns an interview for a work promotion into a shocking pink slip.

Humiliated and effectively homeless, the frazzled woman begrudgingly returns to rural Connecticut and her parents' Greek bakery. But when a fight gets her bounced from the wedding party and she discovers her dad's troubling secrets, Amara wonders if life will always be sour instead of sweet.

Will she ever find the right recipe for happiness?

Reinventing Amara Leventis is a richly drawn women's fiction novel. If you like relatable characters, family dramas, and laugh-out-loud moments, then you'll adore E.D. Hackett's entertaining read.

Farm Cove Bliss

She's relearning to trust. He's healing his heartache. Can Crystal and Derek fix the farmhouse and mend their fractured hearts?

Crystal Whitman is determined to redefine herself. Pulling double shifts to break free from a cheating ex, the single mom worries her life can't get any more chaotic until her own mother dies. The city gal returns to her painfully rural hometown in the hopes of flipping her vacant ancestral farmhouse fast, but she never expected her hunky hired hand would make her want to slow down and enjoy the view.

Derek Fischer can't shake his grief. Twelve years after losing his wife, the devoted dad's broken heart beats only for his daughter, until a sexy school teacher sparks a different kind of love. But with a dying home improvement business to keep afloat, the contractor fears muddling the line between business and pleasure could only end in financial ruin.

When Crystal hires Derek to fix the old farmhouse, so she can sell it and return to her frenzied life, she moves in for the summer to save some money and give him a hand. Fighting their growing attraction, she wonders if she's destined to be alone and he wonders if his wife will ever forgive him for moving on. When a vivacious blonde sinks her claws into Derek, Crystal relives her ex-husbands betrayal, and her reaction could sabotage their growing relationship.

Can these two shattered souls piece together their future and find a happily ever after?

Farm Cove Bliss is a small town sweet romance. If you like small town settings, relatable characters, and mid-life love, you'll adore E.D. Hackett's Farm Cove Bliss.

A Match Made in Ireland

A semester abroad was exactly what she needed, but falling in love with her roommate was not part of the lesson plan.

Rory, an American college student seeking a much-needed break, lands in Ireland for a semester abroad. She never imagines finding her assigned roommate to be Jaime, the charming yet irksome redhead from her flight.

Relying on her lively roommate to act as her personal tour guide, Rory experiences the breathtaking landscapes and Irish traditions that only a local could provide. She falls for more than the enchanting Irish experience he offers and dreams about a life free from worry with someone like Jaime. From kisses in castles to pints in pubs, Rory escapes from the baggage she left behind and envies the carefree life Jaime leads.

Until Rory's ex-boyfriend unexpectedly arrives and feelings of betrayal and doubt erupt. Pulled by past mistakes and newly discovered feelings, she must decide where her future lies. Does her heart belong in Ireland, or was Jaime merely a dream meant to be left behind?

A Match Made in Ireland is a delightful romantic comedy that delves into the magic of Ireland, the beauty of unforeseen bonds, and the transformative power of self-discovery.

Buckle up for a journey filled with laughter, tears, and love that you won't want to miss!

Made in United States
North Haven, CT
04 March 2024